"Don't you w
undressed, A

"Sure I do." His voice was husky, his gaze hot and intense. "But you could have had the decency to wait until I was here to watch."

"Oh." Molly's breasts tingled. Well, of course she should let him watch. Obviously she still had a few things to learn about being a wild woman. "All right, then. Pay attention. I'm going to take off my skirt now."

And she proceeded to take off the garment an inch at a time, making sure her breasts shimmied with every movement. "Enjoying this?" she asked.

Alec looked down at his straining sex, a wry grin on his face. "Obviously."

"Tell you what." She wiggled again, nearly free of the material.

"What?" He was almost fully erect, and it was an impressive sight.

"When I finish this little chore, there might be something else I can do for you...."

She paused, letting the anticipation build. "Do you remember telling me that I had a perfect mouth?" At his dumbfounded nod, Molly slowly ran her tongue over her lips. "Well, what do you say we take it for a test-drive...?"

Dear Reader,

Being chauffeured is a rush, at least for me. Thanks to Harlequin's promotional events, I've had the privilege several times, but one instance in particular stands out. I'd been invited to a reader event at the Beverly Wilshire Hotel, the same place they filmed *Pretty Woman*. Mark Williamson, who met me at LAX, was moonlighting as a chauffeur while waiting for his big break in music. So far, he'd recorded many commercials and one album.

I mentioned Mark to the Harlequin people orchestrating the event, and they hired him for the weekend. On one outing he took us on a tour of Beverly Hills, admitting some time into it that he really didn't know where the stars lived. We didn't care. We listened to his album on the CD player and enjoyed his company. I lost track of Mark after that weekend, but I've always hoped he got the big break he was looking for.

Ever since that experience, I thought a chauffeur would make a terrific hero, and at last Alec Masterson showed up to handle the job. If all chauffeurs looked like Alec, women would burn their driver's licenses. Come along for the ride as Alec does his best (and his best is *awesome*) to drive Molly Drake wild.

Warmly,

Vicki Lewis Thompson

P.S. If you're online, drop by my Web site at www.vickilewisthompson.com and say hello!

Books by Vicki Lewis Thompson

HARLEQUIN TEMPTATION
826—EVERY WOMAN'S FANTASY
853—THE NIGHTS BEFORE
      CHRISTMAS
881—DOUBLE EXPOSURE

HARLEQUIN BLAZE
1—NOTORIOUS
21—ACTING ON IMPULSE
52—TRULY, MADLY, DEEPLY

Vicki Lewis Thompson
DRIVE ME WILD

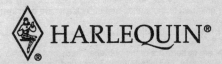

HARLEQUIN®

TORONTO • NEW YORK • LONDON
AMSTERDAM • PARIS • SYDNEY • HAMBURG
STOCKHOLM • ATHENS • TOKYO • MILAN • MADRID
PRAGUE • WARSAW • BUDAPEST • AUCKLAND

For Mark Williamson, who had dreams as big as mine.
I'm still hoping that someday
you'll write the score for my movie!

ISBN 0-373-69121-1

DRIVE ME WILD

1

AS LONG AS Alec Masterson kept driving down the Connecticut Turnpike, he'd pick up his client exactly on time. That meant ignoring the ancient silver Caddy listing to one side on the shoulder up ahead. Now was not the time to play Good Samaritan.

Then a frail old man climbed from behind the wheel and tottered back to the shredded rear tire. Alec groaned and glanced at the clock set into the Lincoln Town Car's leather dash. Nope, couldn't stop. He slowed down, though, hoping somebody else would get out of the Caddy, a teenage grandson, maybe.

If Alec was late, Molly would miss her train into New York, and she'd already told him this trip was important. She hadn't told him why, of course. Molly liked to keep her secrets. His buddy Josh was convinced she starred in X-rated videos. Josh had a wild imagination, but his theory would explain her constant trips to L.A., and she did have an incredible body.

Alec was damn curious but he didn't pry. He was the guy she requested whenever she called the car service, so she must like him. He liked her, too. Lusted after her, in point of fact.

Her red-gold hair seemed designed to fan out on a pillow and her green eyes flashed the kind of fire that gave guys wet dreams. Nevertheless, there was a sweetness, an almost innocent quality to her. If Josh was right about her profession, she was one hell of an actor.

If Alec had met Molly any other way than being her chauffeur, he probably would have asked her out. He had to say *probably* because he really shouldn't take time for a girlfriend right now, and when it came to Molly, he couldn't imagine stopping with one date. But he was her chauffeur, and he couldn't risk losing his job with Red Carpet Limousine.

He'd been playing student for more than ten years, testing out premed, electrical engineering, architecture, accounting. Law school was his last-ditch attempt to find something he loved, and he was determined to finish. The chauffeur's job was perfect—decent money and flexible hours. Plus he could study while he waited for a client.

As Alec passed the Caddy, he checked in the rearview mirror, still hoping to see some able-bodied passenger get out of the car to help the old guy. But no, a tiny, white-haired woman in a pink dress appeared and wobbled to the back of the car. She wore white shoes and carried a white pocketbook. Alec knew that women of her generation called them pocketbooks instead of purses because that was the word his granny used.

Oh, hell. He pulled to the side of the road and backed down the shoulder until he was a couple of yards in front of the Caddy. So he would be late.

MOLLY DRAKE PACED the worn oak floor while keeping an eye on the antique wall clock. Alec was never late, so why now, when this meeting with her agent could mean a new beginning for her? If she missed her eleven-thirty appointment, she wouldn't get in to see Benjamin today. He was a busy man, and she wasn't high enough on the food chain to think he'd squeeze her in somewhere else.

Damn it, where was Alec? She should have learned to drive when she moved to Connecticut. She'd intended to, but Dana had insisted now was not the time, when she was in an unfamiliar place. More protective than Molly's own mother, Dana paid for the car service and told Molly to use it whenever she needed a ride. Privately Molly had planned to learn to drive, anyway, but then Red Carpet Limousine had sent her Alec. Getting a license would have meant giving up Alec, and that was totally unacceptable.

She was positive she wouldn't have written the lust-filled novel sitting on her agent's desk if Alec hadn't come into her life. He'd inspired her to fantasize a grand sexual adventure in which her heroine, Krysta, explored her sensual urges in the primitive jungle setting of Brazil. Molly hadn't ever combed her fingers through Alec's thick brown hair, but Krysta had. Krysta had gazed into his brown eyes while she slowly unbuttoned his silk shirt and rubbed her hands over his muscular chest.

And if he didn't show up in the next two minutes, Molly was going to wring his gorgeous neck. The appointment with Benjamin meant the end of waiting for his reaction to her book. She'd mailed it to him three months ago—three of the most agonizing months of her life. Then last week, his assistant had called to set up this meeting to talk about the book.

Molly was prepared for Benjamin to say he couldn't get her a big advance. Big advances went to Hollywood stars like Dana Kyle, who had astounded Tinseltown by writing a series of clever mysteries. That's what *Publishers Weekly* called them—clever and well plotted.

Molly devoured each review and mailed copies to her parents in L.A. They were the only people besides Benjamin who knew that Molly had ghost-written every word of those mysteries for her dear friend Dana. Dana was thrilled with the recognition, and Molly was happy for her.

But the more famous Dana became, the more she craved participation in the creative process, including face-to-face "brainstorming sessions" with Molly. Molly's brain felt stormed, all right. Dana's ideas were mostly terrible, and Molly had to find diplomatic ways to get out of using them. The process was exhausting, and ended with Dana's name huge on the cover and Molly still invisible. It was time for Molly Drake to appear in print.

Missing this meeting wouldn't be a good beginning. Maybe if Benjamin thought the manuscript was a blockbuster, he might forgive her. She'd had fantasies of that kind of success, of course, but she tried not to get carried away.

Finally she gave in to her impatience, grabbed her large shoulder bag and went outside to wait on the porch. She'd save a couple of minutes if Alec didn't have to knock on the door. She locked up, to save another minute, and sat on the porch swing Grandma Nell used to love so much.

This cottage in Old Saybrook felt more like home than the Beverly Hills mansion where she'd grown up. Even so, she hadn't accepted her grandma's offer of coming to live here because the one-bedroom cottage was so obviously suited for one person and crowded with two.

Maybe she should have come anyway and slept on the couch. At least then she could have spent more time with Grandma Nell before she died. That thought still brought a lump to Molly's throat, but she could think about her grandmother without crying now. The first week she'd lived here, she'd nearly moved away because of the teary spells, but the flood had eased, and now she loved being surrounded by her grandma's antiques, chintz and lace.

Molly nudged the porch floor with her foot and set the swing to moving while she listened for the sound of an engine. Keeping her eye on the spot in the winding road where she'd first be able to see the Town Car's pewter hood, she hoped nothing had happened to Alec. Damn, that hadn't occurred to her until now, and the worry made her stomach twist.

Late was one thing. An accident—well, she didn't even want to think about that. It was a good thing the Town Car was heavy. She'd given her hero a Lincoln, but of course her hero actually owned it, whereas Alec only drove one for Red Carpet. Alec owned an old Blazer, although she'd never seen it.

She willed the Town Car to shove its elegant nose around the bend in the tree-lined road. No such luck. She stopped pumping the swing when she realized how fast she was doing it, as if swinging harder would make him show up. Dreading to see the time, she finally peeked at her watch and panicked. No way would they make it to the station, but that was the least of her worries. Alec wouldn't be this late unless something had happened.

When the phone rang inside the house, she leaped from the swing so fast that it banged against the white clapboard siding. She fumbled in her purse for the key. Finally she located it, unlocked the door and dashed to the phone, a corded model that sat on a little stand in the hall. Her answering machine picked up right as she got there.

She shut the recorder off and snatched up the receiver. "Hello?"

"Molly, I know I'm late, but—"

"Alec! Are you all right?"

"I'm on my way. Listen, you can't make the train now, so I'll drive you to New York. I'll be at your house in five minutes."

"But you're okay, right?"

"Yes, I'm fine." He sounded puzzled. "Why would you think I wasn't?"

"I just...was afraid you might have had an accident or something."

"Oh." There was a brief silence.

In the space of that silence it came to her that maybe she shouldn't have sounded quite so concerned. She'd have to be careful or he might figure out that he was more to her than a chauffeur. And she didn't have time for a real boyfriend. The fantasy kind was much easier to fit into her complicated life.

"I'm sorry," he said. "I didn't mean to worry you. I'll be right there. 'Bye, Molly."

"'Bye." She disconnected the line and stood with the receiver in her hand. His tone had been different at the end, softer, more intimate. Damn it. Sure, she'd flirted with him in the past six months he'd been driving for her, and he'd flirted back. A smart chauffeur would do that to increase his tips, but Molly thought the chemistry between them was real enough. She just didn't want it to get out of hand.

Back in L.A., most of the car services had a policy against dating clients. She knew that because once when she'd been chauffeured to a premiere of her dad's latest movie, the driver had said he'd quit his job if she'd agree to go out with him. Maybe things were different in Connecticut, but she doubted it.

Alec couldn't afford to quit. Besides, he probably didn't have time for a girlfriend any more than she had time for a boyfriend. He was either working or studying. She was either ghost-writing for Dana or stealing hours for her own story.

Okay, that was settled, then. Even if Alec suspected she liked him a lot, and even if he kind of liked her, too, nothing would come of it. The timing was off for both of them.

"Molly?"

She turned to find him standing in the open doorway. She'd dashed inside to answer the phone without closing the door. He had a smudge of grease on his cheek and another one on the front of his white knit shirt with the Red Carpet logo on the breast pocket. His brown eyes held a tenderness that she hadn't seen there before.

"I'm so sorry," he said. "This old couple had a flat tire, and I stopped to help them change it. But you'll still get to your appointment if we leave now, because I can take you right to the door and you won't have to mess around with a taxi at the train station."

She didn't have a lot of choice. "All right. I'll take you up on that." Whenever she saw him her tummy tickled, but this morning that look in his eyes caused the tingling to move a little lower. Good grief, he was turning her on just with a look.

"Good," he said. "Then let's go."

"Right." She put the phone back in its cradle. Her front-door key was still in her right hand, but she had no clue what she'd done with her purse. She glanced around.

"You left it by the front door."

"Oh." She'd been so distracted about Alec that she must have dropped the bag the minute she'd found the house key. "Then I'll just get it and we'll be on our way."

"I left the car running and the air on."

"Great."

He stepped aside and she walked out onto the porch. Sure enough, her purse was lying beside the door, and fortunately nothing had spilled out of it. She locked the cottage door and picked up her bag by the leather strap.

Alec stood at the end of the flagstone walk holding the passenger door open for her, as he'd done countless times before. Long ago they'd dispensed with the tradition of her riding in the back seat. Today Molly wondered if that had been wise. For their own good, they needed to maintain their distance.

But she couldn't very well change the rules now without making things awkward. "Thanks." She slipped into the cool interior of the Town Car, tugging at her short skirt to keep it in place as she avoided his gaze.

She needed to cut way back on the flirtation factor. Deliberately showing a little leg if she happened to be wearing a short skirt or looking into his eyes as she thanked him for holding the door had become second nature. She'd laughed a little too brightly at his jokes and flashed her smile far more than necessary.

Today she could see that behavior had been a mistake. Alec was much too aware of her, and she was absolutely drooling over him. How could she resist a man who was rumpled and late because he'd helped an old couple change a flat tire?

"You're welcome." He swept a glance over her. "Watch your purse strap."

She thought he'd noticed more than the strap, which dangled next to her ankle an inch or so from the door. She pulled it out of the way and he closed the door with a firm thrust.

Firm thrust, indeed. Leave it to her to make closing a car door sexual. It was a habit she might not be able to break—assigning sexual meaning to everything Alec did. That was how she'd been able to imagine him in bed, where firm thrusting would definitely be welcome.

He rounded the hood and opened the driver's door. "How long do you plan to be in the city?"

"Not too long. Why?"

"I could park in a garage and then drive you home." He climbed into the car and closed the door.

"You don't need to do that." Now he was really behaving more like a boyfriend than a chauffeur, and she was enjoying it, unfortunately.

After picking up his sunglasses from the dash and putting them on, he backed out of her small driveway and headed toward the turnpike. "Up to you, but I don't have any other clients today and I'll charge you the same as if you took the train home."

"In that case, sure." She knew he always needed money, and if taking her to New York and back would help him financially, she wouldn't hesitate. "Do you have your books in the trunk?"

He gave her a quick grin. "Always. And I'd much rather have company on the ride back, anyway."

If only he wouldn't smile like that and make her tummy quiver. Until the moment when she'd begun worrying that he'd been in an accident, her emotions regarding him had been under control. But that concern seemed to have eaten away her defenses, and now every move he made created little shock waves in her system.

She groped for solid ground. "You must be getting ready for finals by now."

"Don't remind me." His hands rested easily on the wheel.

"Are you falling behind?" Because she didn't drive, she was fascinated with how casually he handled the big Town Car in heavy traffic. She'd ridden with people who made her nervous, but with Alec she felt completely safe.

He laughed. "I'm always behind, but it's my own fault. Want some music?"

"Okay." With her heightened awareness of him, she wasn't sure music was a good idea, but to say she didn't want any might call attention to a change in their relationship. She hoped by pretending there was no change she'd eventually regain control of her thoughts.

Alec reached over and pushed a button on the CD changer. Obviously he'd preloaded it with soft jazz, their agreed-upon traveling music. In the past, the jazz had filled the car with sensual overtones, but today the atmosphere oozed sex.

For the first time in the six months she'd known Alec, Molly couldn't think of anything to say. Instead, she sat with her fingers laced together and tried to talk herself out of wanting him. She didn't have much luck.

Alec wasn't saying anything, either, and even his silence was sexy. Because they weren't carrying on a conversation, Molly was more aware of his breathing. She had a sudden and powerful image of what it would be like to be lying next to him after.... Her fingers tightened, and she glanced out the window, forcing herself to think of something else, anything else—the budding trees beside the turnpike, the clouds sailing briskly overhead, the flow of traffic down the black ribbon of road.

The trip was an endless exercise in self-control set to a sound track of smoky jazz, but eventually they reached the outskirts of the city, and Molly's thoughts shifted to the appointment with Benjamin. Sexual arousal gave way to a case of nerves.

Alec lowered the volume on the CD player. "So where are we going?"

"Midtown. Near Park and Fifty-seventh." She hesitated. Not telling him anything about their destination, now that he was driving her right to the front door of the building, seemed paranoid. "I have an eleven-thirty appointment with my agent."

Alec nodded. He didn't ask what kind of agent. "Lunch?"

"No, it won't include lunch. I should be finished by twelve-thirty. If you don't mind, maybe we can pick up something to eat on the way home." Right now she had no interest in food, but by then she might be hungry. She hoped she'd be hungry, because that would mean the appointment had gone well.

"Sounds like a plan." Alec's expression remained neutral.

All the questions he wasn't asking hung between them, and she was beginning to feel silly for being so secretive. She couldn't talk about the ghostwriting, but this appointment wasn't connected to that. And after all, he was driving her to Benjamin's office and picking her up again.

Still, no one knew about this project except Benjamin, and she was afraid to talk about it and risk jinxing herself. On the way back to Old Saybrook, though, she'd have a tough time staying silent, especially if Benjamin raved about her writing.

She settled on a compromise. "I'll tell you what this is all about on the way home, okay?"

He glanced at her as if taken aback. "You will? Why?"

"Because I doubt if I'll be able to keep it to myself."

"Then if you'd ridden the train, you would have collared the nearest passenger and blabbed to them?"

Her laugh released some of her nervous energy. "Probably."

"Then I guess I should feel lucky that we missed the train." He sounded irritated.

Whoops. "Look, Alec, I realize I haven't revealed much about myself in the time we've known each other, but—"

"You're not required to reveal anything about yourself, Molly. I apologize for taking that tone. I'm your chauffeur, and what you choose to tell me or not tell me is entirely up to you."

"Now you're upset."

He sighed. "Only with myself. I've known from the beginning that you weren't chatty. And I am."

"Not today."

"Well, I got to thinking that I've probably been boring you. I'll bet you didn't want to hear—"

"I've loved hearing all about your family," she said softly.

"You're being polite."

"No, I'm serious. I don't have any good stories like that." His normal childhood and his adventures with his younger sister made her green with envy.

"Oh, God. Please don't tell me you're an orphan."

"No. But my upbringing was…different."

"And you don't want to talk about it."

"It's better if I don't." She'd discovered a long time ago that nothing good came of telling people her dad was Owen Drake, one of Hollywood's top directors, and her mother was Cybil O'Connor. If fans remembered Cybil O'Connor at all, it was for a spectacular nude scene in *The Haunted Lagoon*, a movie released twenty-eight years ago. After that, she'd given up acting to become Mrs. Owen Drake and mother to Molly Drake. Molly had always felt the weight of that sacrifice.

She'd also learned that mentioning her parents usually brought out intense curiosity, and people tended to forget their manners in the quest for insider dirt. Maybe Alec wouldn't pump her for information about big stars, or mention her mother's infamous nude scene. Knowing Alec, he really wouldn't react that way. Still, Molly liked being anonymous for a change, and moving from L.A. to Connecticut had allowed her to separate herself from that high-pressure, glitzy world.

Alec cleared his throat. "I shouldn't do this, but I have one question about you, and it's killing me."

She braced herself. "Only one?"

"Okay, more than one, but this certain one—let's just say my buddy Josh got me to thinking, and I can't get the question out of my head."

"Is Josh the driver I met when you gave him a ride?"

"Yeah, when his limo broke down outside New Haven."

Molly remembered a wiry guy with curly black hair. Josh always seemed to be in motion. "A high-energy type."

"That's the one. Anyway, you don't have to answer,

but if you could say yes or no, it would mean a lot to me."

"You sound as if this has been keeping you up at night."

Alec coughed. Then he coughed again, and the tips of his ears grew pink. "Uh, no, not really."

She couldn't make sense of his reaction until she replayed what she'd said. *You sound as if this has been keeping you up at night.* When she realized the potential double meaning, heat rushed to her face, too. "Wait a minute. I wasn't trying to be—"

"Are you in the movies?"

Startled, she laughed. She was so not in the movies. Her parents had wanted that more than anything, and she'd tried. But an introverted little bookworm, no matter what she looked like on the outside, couldn't expect to make it on the big screen, even with a stage-door mommy *and* a stage-door daddy.

"Are you?"

She smiled at him. This conversation was helping her case of nerves. "Well, you caught me. I'm not Molly Drake at all. I'm really Nicole Kidman trying to escape the paparazzi."

"Um, I didn't mean that kind of movie."

"Then what—" Her mouth dropped open. Alec was asking her if she acted in adult videos.

"But I'll bet Josh has it all wrong."

At first she was insulted that Alec would think it was remotely possible that she was a porn star. He should know her better than that. Or should he? She hadn't talked about herself, which left room for all kinds of speculation. Apparently Josh and Alec thought she looked sexy enough to act in those videos, which intrigued her. "You said I didn't have to answer, right?"

"Of course you don't have to answer, but—"

"So I'm not going to." Then she watched the pink that had tinged his ears make its way over his entire face. Darting a glance into his lap, she discovered that the image of her as an X-rated video star was having quite an effect on him there, too.

His voice sounded strangled. "So you are."

"I didn't say that." This was fascinating, and it definitely kept her mind off her anxiety-producing appointment with Benjamin.

"Yeah, but not answering is the same as answering."

"Not necessarily." She wondered what he'd do if she put a hand on his thigh, but she didn't want them to have an accident.

"Now I wish I hadn't asked." He swallowed. "I thought you'd say no."

"That's no fun."

"Oh, so you really aren't, but you want me to think you are?"

Highly entertained, she continued to smile at him. "What do you think?"

He gripped the steering wheel and stared at the road ahead. "I think I just got myself into a heap of trouble."

2

ALEC NEEDED A COLD SHOWER, but that wasn't possible, so he casually adjusted the air-conditioning vent so it blew directly on his lap. He'd been worried that the X-rated video question would insult Molly, but at least then he'd have had his answer. She wasn't insulted. She was taking the Fifth.

Even if he hadn't studied law, he'd still know that anybody who refused to answer was most likely hiding something. So she really could be a star of those movies. He wasn't proud of his reaction to the news, either. Damned if he wasn't rising to the occasion.

She could also be teasing him. That concept didn't improve his condition at all. A woman willing to kid around about something like that would be the kind of bed partner he'd always dreamed of, someone who liked to have fun with sex instead of making it into a serious business. She was either an X-rated movie star or a sexy little tease. Both possibilities had him so turned on he could barely drive the car.

But that's what she was paying him to do, and he'd better stop fantasizing about her naked body or they'd find themselves in a ten-car pileup in Midtown. He glanced over at her, trying to decide if she was kidding him or not.

She just smiled, as if watching him squirm was giving her great pleasure. She certainly didn't dress as if she made that kind of movie. Sure, her skirt was on the short side, but it belonged to a black silk suit that looked more *Glamour* than *Playboy*. His sister subscribed to *Glamour*, and she'd be very impressed with the outfit Molly was wearing.

Then again, an X-rated star wouldn't necessarily dress the part when she wasn't in front of the camera. Molly's outfit didn't tell him much except that she had good taste in clothes. Damn, he didn't know what to think. And with a large portion of his blood draining south, he didn't have much left to power his brain, anyway.

Somehow he managed to follow Molly's directions and get her to the right address. He even remembered to give her his cell-phone number so that she could call him when she was finished. Then, like an idiot, he sat and watched her go into the building. If he hadn't been startled out of his trance by blaring horns and New York–style swearing, he might have stayed right there until she showed up again.

Humbled by what a complete moron he'd turned into, he drove to the nearest parking garage, found a space and leaned back against the headrest with a sigh. He never should have asked her. Instead of satisfying his curiosity, she'd made herself more mysterious and fascinating than ever. His overheated brain buzzed with thoughts of Molly, sex kitten. Something told him he wouldn't get much studying done in the next hour.

MOLLY SAT in the red leather chair in Benjamin's office. Her manuscript, bound by a thin rubber band, lay on the desk between them. Benjamin gazed at her from behind his thick glasses. His gray hair was carefully combed. He wasn't smiling.

Looking at him, Molly decided she didn't want to talk about the manuscript. She might not ever want to talk about the manuscript. "It really feels like spring out there," she said. "I didn't even need a coat. Is it usually this warm in April?"

"Not usually. Listen, I've read your manuscript, and I—"

"I've never spent a whole summer in this area. I'm looking forward to walking on the beach, buying produce from roadside stands, getting a—"

"Molly, I'm sorry."

She felt as if someone had shoveled ice cubes into her stomach. "The book, um, needs work?" She cleared her throat. "That's okay. I can—"

"I wish I could believe that you can fix it."

She stared at him. "Of course I can fix it! I'm a professional writer, so tell me what needs to be done, and I'll do it." Maybe this was a nightmare and she'd wake up. She pinched her arm, but nothing changed. She was still sitting in a chair across from a very sad-looking, gray-haired agent who didn't like her book.

"I assume that you want this to be a hot read about a woman exploring her sexual fantasies."

"Well, that's sort of what I was going for." And Benjamin didn't think she'd pulled it off. She swallowed. Life didn't get much more hideous than this, having a middle-aged man tell you that when it came to sex, you just didn't get it. Benjamin's blue eyes looked huge and filled with sympathy. She didn't want sympathy. She wanted the *New York Times* bestseller list with Molly Drake in the top ten.

"It's not sexy," he said, putting an unnecessary point on what had been, up to now, merely hinted at.

She winced. But hey, what did Benjamin know, anyway? He'd been married since Nixon was president. He probably couldn't remember what sex was like!

Benjamin folded his hands and leaned toward her. "I don't think writing about sex is your strong point. The cozy mysteries you've been writing for Dana—that's where you need to put your energy. They don't require any sex."

"I'm sick of writing cozy mysteries!"

"Then maybe you need a break. You've been turning out those books for Dana faster than you should. I can have that August deadline moved, if you want me to. Dana's established, now, so you can—"

"That's exactly it." Molly hadn't realized how much this manuscript meant to her until now, when Benjamin seemed ready to dump it in his stylish trash can. *"Dana's* established. I'm not. I'm grateful for her, grateful for the money, but I want to publish something under my own name."

Benjamin sighed and leaned back in his chair. "You're in a catch-22, then, because it can't be anything similar to what you're writing for her. There's that noncompete clause in the contract."

Molly gestured toward the manuscript on his desk. "That's not similar."

"No. But if you'd hoped to leap to another genre, I'm afraid you didn't quite succeed."

Her heart was beating like a jackhammer. She wanted to believe that Benjamin didn't know what he was talking about, but he had some clients who wrote hot books. Obviously he didn't think she fit in with those authors. Later on she'd probably cry about this, but right now she was too busy fighting for her creative life to cry. "I'll rewrite the love scenes."

"I don't know if that will work."

"Of course it will. I thought they were sexy enough, but apparently I was wrong. I'll do something about that."

He gazed at her for several long seconds. "I don't know how to say this, so I'll probably say it wrong, but the manuscript reads as if the author doesn't have much experience with the concept of sexual adventure."

She sat in stunned silence.

"That's why I doubt you can fix it," he added gently. "Again, my advice is to stick with the cozy mysteries. Let's face it, Molly, you're a cautious person, a basically introverted person, which many writers are. This kind of book just isn't you. Cozy mysteries fit you perfectly."

Molly's ears rang as blood rushed to her head. This was unacceptable. This was totally unacceptable. How ironic that Alec half believed that she was an X-rated video star and Benjamin saw her as introverted and sexually timid. She wasn't sexually timid! She just...okay, maybe she was a wee bit cautious when it came to sex, but she was far from a virgin.

She hadn't had much experience because she hadn't relished having her sexual exploits splashed all over the tabloids. As a result, she might have reined herself in too much. But under the right circumstances, she was certainly capable of throwing caution to the winds and grabbing life by the *cojones*. If that would inspire better sex scenes, she'd do it.

"Of course, I'll send it out if you insist," Benjamin said. "You have the final say-so."

"No." Molly stood and plucked the manuscript from his desk. The rubber band broke, and she had to grab the stack of pages with both hands to keep them from scattering all over Benjamin's tidy office. "I'll take what you said under advisement."

Benjamin stood, too. "Molly, do you know how many writers would kill to be in your shoes? Not very many people make a living at writing, you know."

"I do know." She stuffed the manuscript into her shoulder bag. Once she got it home she'd treat it more carefully, like the wounded child it was, but for now she wanted to make her exit. "I'm grateful for the chance Dana's given me. But I will publish something under my own name."

"I'm sure you will." Benjamin was old enough to be her father and unfortunately he was beginning to sound uncomfortably like a father. "You just need to find the right vehicle."

"I just need to find more sex!" The moment the words came out, Molly blushed. But it was true. And she needed to work on controlling that blush if she intended to reinvent herself.

Benjamin looked uncomfortable. "Wait a minute, Molly. Don't think for a minute that I'm advocating that you—"

"I don't think that."

He continued to eye her uneasily. "People can't change their basic personality, and if they try, they can get into big trouble."

"Absolutely." Except her personality wasn't quite as basic as Benjamin thought. Maybe she needed more knowledge, but she'd loved putting together that book, amateurish as it might have turned out to be. She was a sexual diamond in the rough. And she had some ideas as to how to acquire that all-important polish.

He smiled in obvious relief. "I'm glad you're not planning to do anything rash. It's a dangerous world out there, and you have to be careful."

"Exactly." She wondered if Benjamin had a clue what

it was like "out there," but he was trying to protect her, which was sweet. Considering that she wasn't a big-deal client, only the ghostwriter for a big-deal client, she should probably be flattered that he cared about her well-being.

"Well, then." Benjamin clasped his hands together. "Would you like me to have that August deadline changed so you can have a breather?"

"No, that's okay." Molly didn't want Dana to get an inkling that her ghostwriter was dissatisfied with the status quo. When Molly was a teenager and had wanted to ditch the acting gig in order to write, Dana had taken her side against her mom and dad. Molly intended to treat Dana right.

"So you're okay, then?" He looked as if he needed reassurance.

"I'm fine." She managed a smile. "Thank you for reading the manuscript."

"Parts of it were excellent."

"Thank you." She resisted the urge to ask him which parts. Whether or not she could write wasn't the issue. The question was whether or not she could write about raw, uninhibited sex.

They shook hands and said their goodbyes. As Molly made her way out of his office, she dug through her purse for the business card with Alec's cell phone number on it. Thanks to a buddy with a wild imagination, Alec thought she might be a woman who acted out sex scenes in front of a camera. That obviously turned him on. She was about to trade shamelessly on that piece of misinformation.

ALEC WAS AMAZED when Molly called him before twelve-thirty. If he'd had an hour-long appointment with her, he'd have used the entire sixty minutes. For some reason her agent had let her get away early. Must be a woman.

Traffic was dense, but traffic was always dense in New York. Other than wanting to pick up Molly ASAP, Alec didn't mind fighting traffic. Actually, he enjoyed the challenge. In the city he pictured himself as Luke Skywalker shooting through the Death Star maze. On the turnpike he pretended to drive the Indy 500, but he had to watch out for that fantasy. Too many speeding tickets and he'd be out of a job.

Molly was standing on the sidewalk where he'd left her, and she didn't look very happy. She'd promised to tell him about this meeting, though, so he'd find out what or who had put that expression on her face. He didn't like seeing Molly unhappy and took an instant dislike to her agent, who probably was responsible for making her sad.

He doubled-parked and got out to open the door for her, but she was inside before he made it all the way around the car. Molly was like that, not the least interested in being treated like a diva. She didn't know that he loved opening doors for her.

"Let's have lunch at a hotel," she said the minute he got behind the wheel.

"Which one?"

"Any one. The closest one. My treat. Use valet parking. I'm really hungry."

"Okay." He doubted this was a celebration, but he wasn't going to argue with her. If she wanted a nice meal in a hotel restaurant, he'd make sure she got it. He wished he could offer to buy her lunch, but at New York prices, lunch could suck up a good portion of his rent money. He'd never minded being poor until this moment.

He drove around the block and pulled into the valet parking area of the first high-rise hotel he came to, not even bothering to notice if it was a Hilton, Sheraton or something else entirely.

"Perfect." She was helped out of the car by the doorman while Alec gave the keys to the parking attendant.

As Alec walked over to join her, he remembered he was dressed in his car service logo shirt, which was smudged. "Maybe you should go in without me," he said. "I'm not wearing the right clothes."

She glanced at him. "You're fine, but if you're worried about it, we can go to the hotel coffee shop instead of the dining room."

He followed her through the revolving doors. "It depends on what you want to eat."

"I'd rather be in the coffee shop with you than by myself in the dining room. Let's get a sandwich."

He was a little confused by her strange mood, but he decided to play along. "Okay." As they walked through the lobby on their way to the coffee shop, he caught a glimpse of the two of them in a large wall mirror. With her dressed in elegant city clothes and him in his chauffeur's outfit, he sure did look like her boy toy.

He wondered if she had boy toys. In the six months he'd known her, he hadn't seen evidence that she dated anyone. That didn't mean much, though. Logically she wouldn't need a chauffeur when a guy was around, so he wouldn't have reason to cross paths with her dates.

The hostess showed them to a table, and Alec held Molly's chair for her.

She smiled up at him. "Thanks."

"I should be thanking you, for offering to buy my

lunch." He sat down, picked up the menu and glanced at the prices. The place was fancy for a coffee shop, but there were a few meals in his price range. "You know, I could pay for my own. That makes more sense."

"Let's not worry about it now." She made quick work of studying the menu and was ready for the waiter when he came to fill their water glasses.

While she ordered a grilled-chicken salad, Alec quickly decided on a Reuben. Once the waiter left, Alec leaned forward. "You said you'd tell me about your meeting with your agent."

"I will, but not right this minute." Her green eyes were bright, her cheeks flushed. The sad expression had disappeared.

"I take it she didn't give you good news."

"It's *he*, and no, he didn't. But I don't intend to let that spoil our meal. So you like Reuben sandwiches?"

"Sure do."

"So do I, but I felt like having something a little lighter. Maybe you'll let me have a bite of yours."

This was feeling more and more like a date. "Uh, sure."

"There's something about that tangy combo of sauerkraut and corned beef, isn't there?"

"I've always liked it."

"And if they bring it immediately after they fix it, and it's still warm, with the cheese melted...mmm, yummy."

"Uh-huh." He had the definite impression this discussion was about something besides food. His groin was registering sexual overtones. Major sexual overtones. Molly had flirted with him before, but it had been more on the order of Sex Lite, not really intended to go anywhere. This time she seemed to have a definite destination in mind, and he was getting hotter by the second.

"Alec?"

He cleared his throat. "What?"

"I'll bet Red Carpet has a policy against dating clients."

His heart started beating faster. "It does. But if you're worried about this lunch, I don't think that counts. I mean, you have to eat." He'd pretend to misunderstand where the conversation was leading, to see if she was serious or messing with his head.

"I wasn't really worried about this lunch. We're in New York, not Old Saybrook. No one will see us having lunch, whether your company would frown on it or not."

"I guess that's true."

"So, let's say you decided to take a chance, decided for a little while to ignore your company's policy. Let's say your client promised never to say anything to anyone." She paused to gaze at him.

If he hadn't noticed the slight tremor of her hand as she reached for her water glass, he would have thought she was cool as can be. He wasn't, though. He was breaking out in a sweat. "Okay, let's say that."

She sloshed a little water over the rim of the glass as she set it unsteadily back on the tablecloth. Her eyelashes fluttered, and then she looked straight at him. "I don't want you to lose your job on account of me."

"You let me worry about that." He no longer gave a damn about the job. Five minutes ago he'd thought it was very important, but five minutes ago Molly hadn't been across the table, color high, hinting that she wanted something more from him than chauffeur service.

"It's just that I find you very attractive," she said.

"Ditto." That was suave. He tried again. "I find you very attractive, too."

"But there are so many problems."

"I know." He couldn't think of a single one, but he knew they were out there, temporarily obliterated by a firestorm of lust.

"I don't really have time for dating." She gripped the slick water glass in both hands and brought it to her mouth for a single swallow.

So she hadn't been going out, after all. Nice to know. "Why not?"

"I'm trying to move ahead in my career."

Making X-rated movies? But he didn't ask. "I don't really have time to date, either." He said it automatically, but now he realized that he'd make the time—for her.

"That's what I thought. And then there's the situation with me being a client for the car service."

"True." And maybe he'd been crazy to let that stand in his way for six months. Was he a man or a wuss?

She turned the water glass around and around in her hands while she stared at the ice bobbing inside. "But that doesn't mean I haven't thought about it."

"So have I." Which answered the question of whether he was a man or a wuss. He'd thought about her during the day, dreamed about her at night, and hadn't made a single move. Pathetic.

But most of their time together had been side by side, riding in the Town Car. This was the longest he'd ever sat across from her, able to really look at her. She was a treat, all red-gold curls and creamy skin.

He'd never noticed her hands before, but he noticed them now as she continued to fondle her water glass. She kept her nails short and free of polish. Movie stars, any kind of movie star, had long nails. But she could put on the fake ones during shooting. He was fascinated by the way she was stroking that dripping glass. Then she clutched it in two hands again and took another sip. God, he was getting hard.

She took a long, shaky breath. "Okay, so we're both interested."

"Definitely."

"And fate has caused us to end up in the city together today."

"Yes." Fate in the form of George and Alma Federman, whose flat tire had made him late. They'd insisted on inviting him over for dinner some night this week, but he should be the one taking them out, from the look of things.

"So, um, I was thinking..."

His heart thudded like a pile driver. "Yes?"

"Well, considering everything—" She stopped and glanced up as the waiter appeared with their food.

Alec wasn't hungry anymore. He wanted her to keep talking. The waiter seemed to take forever setting down the plates, asking if they needed anything, getting ketchup for the fries that had come with his Reuben.

Finally they were alone again. "You were saying?" Alec prompted.

"I think we should eat." She picked up her fork, but her hand was still trembling.

"Is this the date? Lunch?"

"Eat your Reuben."

"I mean, we could take a walk through Central Park, or something like that." Then he worried that he sounded cheap. Unfortunately he didn't have much cash on him, and his credit card didn't have a whole lot of room on it, either.

"Before we decide what we're going to do, we should eat our food." She speared some chicken and lettuce with her fork.

"Okay." He dutifully took a bite of his Reuben. He'd never realized before how juicy a Reuben was. It dripped on his fingers and he ended up licking them. Then he glanced up and found her watching him, her lips parted, her breathing uneven.

"Is it good?" she asked.

"Yes." Oh, man, she was delectable. "Want some?"

She nodded.

He held out the sandwich, putting his other hand underneath to catch the drips. When she leaned over to take a bite, her lips brushed his fingers. Just in time he stifled a groan.

She chewed and swallowed. "It is good."

"You can have the rest." *You can have anything you want.* He picked up his plate to give it to her.

"No. No, thank you. I have my salad." She started eating it again as if someone had told her she couldn't have dessert unless she cleaned her plate.

Alec decided he might as well follow her lead, so he polished off half the sandwich. But as he was tackling the other half, he decided to get this money situation out in the open. "I like your idea of spending time together here in New York today, and I wish I could afford to take you somewhere nice, maybe even to a matinee on Broadway, but I don't have much—"

"Alec, I'll cover the cost of whatever we do."

"That doesn't feel right. I know it's a new century, but I want to at least pay my own way."

"When do you have to have the car back?"

"Sometime tonight. Edgars doesn't need it until tomorrow, and I have access to the parking lot, so there's no deadline or anything. We can hang around the city as long as you want."

She hadn't finished her salad, but she pushed her plate away. "I don't want to hang around the city."

"But you said—"

"I want..." She paused and lowered her voice. "I want to get a room."

Alec almost came in his pants.

3

MOLLY'S FACE FELT HOT, but she'd said the words. Not elegantly, not seductively, but clearly.

Alec's brown eyes turned almost black. "You're propositioning me," he said, his voice hoarse.

"Yes." She gripped the edge of the table as she waited for his answer.

"I'd be a fool to turn down an offer like that. But if you're thinking of this hotel, then I'm afraid the cost is beyond my—"

"I'll pay for the room."

"No."

"Listen to me." She reached over and grabbed his hand. Now that she'd started down this road, she wasn't turning back. She'd never grabbed a man's hand before in her life, but from the way Alec gripped her fingers, it was the right move. "Taking a room here is the perfect solution. No one ever has to know about it."

He captured her hand between both of his. "I'll feel like a gigolo, Molly. Believe me, I love that you asked, but it's like you'd be paying me for sex."

"I would not!" She was thrilled with the masterful way he'd taken over the hand-holding business, but she didn't want his ego to get in the way of what she had in mind. "I'm only paying for the room so we can be alone together."

"Same thing."

She had to admit that if she paid, the balance of power was in her favor. For a—what had Benjamin called her? A cautious introvert?—assuming that power was a huge step. She needed to do it in order to lay claim to the sexual adventurer buried deep in her soul.

But first she had to convince Alec to stop being so macho. She thought of how she'd handle him if he were a character in one of her books. In order to get him to change his mind, she'd have to introduce new information. It worked in fiction.

"I need to let you know something," she said.

"Shoot." His tone was casual, but a pulse was beating rapidly in his throat.

"Josh is wrong. I'm not an X-rated video star. I'm not in the movies at all."

He gripped her hand tighter. "You sure look like you could be."

"Thank you. But looks can be deceiving. I'm almost the opposite of that."

He drew in a quick breath. "A virgin?"

"No." Was that a gasp of excitement or anxiety? "Would that matter to you?"

"Molly, that kind of thing *always* matters. But to be honest, if you'd gone all this time without having sex, I'd be a little worried about you."

"Well, I'm not going to pretend I've had tons of experience, either."

The lines of determination softened, and he smiled. "That's okay."

"I'm not normally this bold."

His grip on her hand loosened enough for him to stroke her palm with his thumb. "That's what I thought, but Josh gets an idea in his head and he can be very convincing."

His touch was subtle, but erotic all the same. She'd chosen quickly, but she'd chosen well. Alec would definitely expand her sexual horizons. Her heart thumped crazily as she imagined what the afternoon might bring. "The thing is, I don't think I've ever reached my...my full potential, sexually speaking. But I'm hoping that if the setting is right, and the man is right, I can learn to let go."

He swallowed, his gaze welded to hers.

She forged on. "The setting I've always imagined is a luxurious hotel room, an escape from the world where it won't matter who we are."

"Like this place." His voice rasped with tension.

"Exactly like this. Alec, I've been dreaming about you for months. Spending a few stolen hours in a room in this hotel with a man like you would be a fantasy come true."

He took a shaky breath. "That's a lot of pressure. What if I disappoint you?"

"I'm more worried that I'll disappoint you."

"Not possible."

"Sure it is." She faced her worst fear. "Maybe I'm wrong about myself. Maybe I won't be able to let go and be wild and crazy."

"Have you ever...um...had an—"

"Yes. Everything works." And each time, she'd been left with the feeling that it should be easier, better, more world-shattering. "But I've never been...well, turned inside out."

He blew out a puff of air. "Now I'm intimidated. No way am I going to sit here and promise you that I'll be able to do that."

"I'm not asking you to." She quivered with anticipation. "I'm only asking you to try."

AS ALEC LOOKED into Molly's eyes, he reminded himself to breathe. What a rush, knowing she wanted him so much, but the prospect was scary as hell, the possibility of failure huge.

He'd always wanted to sky-dive, but hadn't had the money or the opportunity. Or maybe he'd used the money problem as an excuse because he'd been too damn scared and couldn't admit that, even to himself. He imagined his first jump would feel something like this—adrenaline pumping, fear mixed in with wild anticipation and the knowledge that he'd never forgive himself if he chickened out and didn't jump.

He still didn't like the financial arrangements surrounding this episode, but he understood why she'd want the fancy, anonymous hotel room. She planned to pretend she was someone else for a few hours in hopes she'd lose her inhibitions. He was the lucky guy who'd been asked to assist in that.

That put a lot of pressure on his ability to perform, but he'd have to get over that. Somehow. He was glad she wasn't an X-rated video star. Knowing that she was an unfulfilled woman looking for a peak experience was less scary than thinking she created images of sexual ecstasy for a living. Molly was asking him to help her, and he'd always been a sucker for a person in need of help.

Yeah, right. He was a noble person, all right, devoting his time to her cause. Not. But he was surprised at how much courage it took to agree to her plan. He took a deep breath. "Okay," he said. "I'm willing to try."

Her cheeks got all rosy and her smile trembled at the corners. "Good."

"On the condition you let me buy lunch." He'd use his credit card, much as he hated to keep adding to the amount he couldn't seem to pay off. Maybe he could pull some double shifts later this month for extra cash.

"That's silly."

"Not to me." He would also repay her for the cost of the hotel room. If that meant dipping into the stash he was accumulating toward next year's tuition, so be it.

"All right. While you're paying for lunch, I'll go back to the lobby and book the room."

He nodded and released her hand. "That works." He'd rather not be there when she plopped down her gold card for the room, anyway. "Then you'll come back here?"

"Yes, but only to drop off the key folder for you. Then I'll go on up to the room alone, and you can follow later."

His insecurities hit him again. "Because of the way I'm dressed?"

"Oh, no. I love the way you're dressed. But somebody has to buy condoms."

"Oh." He felt the blush coming and hated it. "Well, I knew that." He'd forgotten totally, and he was a man who *never* forgot that particular item. He wondered if he could have ended up poised on the brink of paradise only to discover he was condomless. Could be. His brain wasn't working very well at the moment.

"Then I'll be back in a little bit." She picked up her purse and left the coffee shop.

He was facing away from the exit, so he couldn't watch her leave. Instead, he had to sit there, sip his water and hope he looked relaxed and casual, as if he took part in scenes like this all the time. Because he didn't, he'd better start with a little advance planning.

First of all, he'd buy her a single rose. Nice touch. When he walked into the room, he'd approach her slowly and present the rose. He'd look deeply into her eyes, and then he'd kiss her. The kiss should last a long time. If he intended to drive her wild, he should draw out the process.

Yeah, the key was to keep it slow and build the tension gradually. He could do that. Then he suddenly realized that he needed to get the waiter over to the table with the check. He caught the guy's attention and motioned to him.

The waiter hurried over. "Everything okay, sir?"

"Everything's fine." *Everything's incredible, except that I've been propositioned by an amazing woman and I'm scared to death that I won't live up to her expectations.* "I'd like the check, please."

"Certainly."

While the man was gone, Alec took out his wallet and counted the bills to make sure he had enough cash for the condoms and the single red rose.

"Here you are, sir." The waiter left a leather folder beside Alec's plate. "Would you like me to box any of that for you?"

Alec hated to see the food go to waste, but he couldn't picture himself arriving at the door of Molly's room with a red rose and a doggie bag. "No, thanks." He stuck his credit card in the leather folder and handed it to the waiter. "Where's the florist shop?"

"Right off the main lobby and to your left."

Alec's plans were shaping up. After a very long kiss, he'd take the rose, lay it...somewhere, and begin to undress her. Maybe she'd take off her clothes and climb into bed before he arrived. That might make his slow seduction a little tougher. But ripping off his clothes and jumping into bed with her lacked class.

God, he hoped he didn't make a complete fool of himself. For one thing, he hadn't had sex in several months. Even that had been a short-term event, because Sharon hadn't appreciated working around his demanding schedule. The chemistry hadn't been great, so he'd let her slip away without an argument.

But the chemistry with Molly was off the charts. Considering how much he wanted her and how celibate he'd been recently, he could have a problem with control. He hoped not. Control was another key ingredient if he planned to do as she'd asked and turn her inside out. Yep, control was essential, and—he jumped when he heard her voice just over his shoulder.

"I have the key," she said softly. Then she moved into his field of vision and stood hesitantly beside the table.

He pushed back his chair and stood. "What next?"

"I don't want to make a production of giving it to you."

"Then wait until we leave the coffee shop." He gestured toward the food. "Do you want to take any of this?"

She glanced at their plates. "You know, we should probably get a doggie bag. We might be hungry... after."

Lust surged through him, leaving him trembling. Doggie bags. Doggie style. They would eat the rest of this food while they were naked. Omigod. *Easy does it, sport. Slow down. Control. It's all about being slow and in control.*

When the waiter came back with the credit card slip, Alec said they'd changed their minds and wanted the food boxed. The waiter whisked the plates away while Alec stared at the slip of paper and tried to remember his name.

"It's too expensive," Molly said. "Let me pay for it."

"It's not too expensive. I was deciding how much of a tip to leave."

She rummaged in her purse. "I'll leave the tip."

He caught her wrist. "No, you won't. Let me salvage a little of my male pride."

Her glance was soft with understanding. "I really don't mean to insult you. It's only that this is my idea, so I think I should—"

"I've had this idea ever since the day I met you."

Her eyes widened. "You have?"

"You couldn't tell?"

"I thought you were being nice so you'd get better tips."

"I would have driven you around for free." He took the plastic bag containing their food from the outstretched hand of the waiter. "Thanks." Then he turned back to Molly. "Speaking of that, what happens after today? I don't see how I can continue to be your driver, do you?" *Unless we end every trip in the back seat, naked.*

She looked startled. "I...I hadn't thought of that."

"Maybe you should." Maybe he should. Although he was ready to trade one afternoon of making love to Molly for future months of driving her around, he would really miss her. Yet he couldn't imagine how they could go back to being strictly client and chauffeur. But if they kept fooling around on the side, his boss would find out, and all hell would break loose.

When she stood there looking confused and not saying anything, he took her arm and guided her out of the coffee shop. "Maybe we need to sit in the lobby and talk about this. It's not too late to back out."

"Yes, it is. I've asked you to have sex with me. We couldn't possibly pretend I'd never done that."

"We'd have a much better chance of pretending if we don't go upstairs. But going upstairs is pretty much going to blow the lid off any chance of maintaining the status quo."

She turned, looking adorably troubled as she faced him. "Do you want to back out?"

"I—"

"Sir!"

Alec turned as the waiter rushed out, heading their way. The bottom dropped out of Alec's stomach as he imagined that his credit card had been rejected for being over the limit. He'd thought he had room, but maybe not.

"You forgot your card," the waiter said.

That was only marginally better. He was solvent, but he'd managed to look like a moron in front of a woman he wanted to impress with his coolness. "Thank you." He took the card and shoved it into his pants pocket. No, he wasn't rattled. Not him. Not much.

"I'm glad they discovered it now," Molly said after the waiter left.

"I can't believe I left it there. You must think I'm—"

"I think you're nervous. Like me."

He looked into her eyes and thought that he hadn't done that nearly enough in the past six months. If they went through with this, he might have a few more hours of that privilege, and then he'd probably have to give her up. "Could be. This is a big step we're contemplating."

"Do you want to reconsider?"

"Molly, I want it all. I want this afternoon, and I want to keep being your driver." *And your lover.*

She nodded, making her red-gold curls bounce. "Me, too. That's what I want."

"But it's not realistic." In that moment he knew his choice. Reckless urges rolled through him. Right here in the middle of the lobby he was tempted to bury his fingers in her hair and pull her close so he could kiss those full lips. "You're the one in charge. You need to choose." *Choose this. Choose making love until we can't see straight. Let tomorrow take care of itself.*

Her gaze searched his. "Then I choose this afternoon."

His pulse leaped. "You're sure?"

"I want to find out who I become when...when you hold me."

His brain stalled, immobilized by that seductive image. "Oh, Molly."

"I'm going up now." She tucked the key folder inside the plastic bag of food. "I'll see you soon."

SHE'D STARTED OUT wanting to have an afternoon of wild sex with Alec so she could begin to improve her writing. Somewhere along the way her motivation had changed to something else. Now she wanted this not only for her writing, but for herself.

Although she'd never been part of the anything-goes crowd in Hollywood, she'd secretly envied those free spirits. Here was her chance to cut loose without the danger of the paparazzi showing up. She deserved to know what she was capable of sexually, and she believed Alec was the man who could show her.

That didn't mean she was filled with confidence as she rode the elevator to the ninth floor and located the room down a carpeted hallway. Growing up in an un-inhibited atmosphere, she'd protected her sensitive soul by wearing her own inhibitions like a suit of armor. The thought of shedding it scared her to death.

She'd also spent a lifetime, except for her visits to Connecticut, being recognized as the daughter of a celebrity. That feeling was hard to shake, and she imagined that anyone seeing her would know immediately what she planned to do with her afternoon. Thankfully she passed no one on the way.

She'd never checked into a hotel for one night without a bit of luggage, either. At the desk she'd made up a story of suitcases lost by the airline, but she didn't think the clerk had believed her. Her stuttering over the explanation hadn't helped.

Well, here she was, key card in hand, standing in front of the door to a whole new world. She had the urge to run the other way. But then she would miss this perfect opportunity to become the woman who'd peeked out from the pages of her manuscript, a woman who wanted more than mediocre sex.

If she didn't follow through with her plan, she might be doomed to write cozy mysteries for Dana Kyle forever. Worse yet, she'd have blown her chance to discover, after countless hours of imagining, what the flesh-and-blood Alec was like in bed. She might never find another man who fueled her fantasies the way he did. He'd inspired her to write an entire book without laying a hand on her. Once they'd made love, she might never stop typing.

Straightening her spine, she slid the key card into the slot, waited for the blinking green light and opened the door. The room was furnished in dark woods and pseudo-antiques. A four-poster bed held a luxury mattress and box springs that elevated the top edge to about...crotch height. Of course she'd think of that. Pulse racing, she closed the door and automatically flipped the privacy latch into place. Then she remembered that Alec had to be able to get in and switched it back.

Her stomach did a few flips as she realized he could be here any minute, and the room looked far too prissy to be the scene of a wild seduction. Walking quickly over to the high bed, she tossed back the covers. Better. Then she pulled the drapes and turned on one lamp in the corner, across the room from the bed. There would be light, but not a glare.

Kicking off her shoes, she pulled up her skirt and shoved down her panty hose. Absolutely nothing was less sexy than panty hose. They didn't look sexy going on or off, so she shoved them into her purse, not wanting to spoil the mood by tugging them back on later.

God, she was trembling like a leaf. Deep breaths. She paused and dragged in air until she started getting light-headed. Okay, that wasn't working.

Think, Molly. Think. What else should she do to get ready? Take off everything and get into bed? No, she wanted to find out if Alec knew how to undress a woman. Her fantasy included a man who could navigate buttons and zippers with finesse, while making it perfectly clear that he'd rather tear her clothes off.

However, she had a competing fantasy in which a man wallowed in his baser instincts and sent buttons scampering over the carpet as he uncovered what he was after. She imagined his deep groan of impatience and the satisfying rip of delicate material by hands trembling with passion. Unfortunately, leaving the hotel in an outfit that had been reduced to rags wasn't part of her fantasy, so she'd better make sure Alec didn't ruin her clothes in a fit of lust.

Maybe she should give him a little head start on the process. At least the shoes and the panty hose were gone. She studied herself in the mirror. Her silk suit jacket was meant to stay buttoned, and underneath she wore a really boring bra.

She'd been thinking about that bra ever since she'd had the idea of seducing Alec today. When she'd picked that one out of the drawer this morning, she'd been going for comfort. She'd expected to spend the day riding the train, not cavorting in a hotel room with Alec. The debate of comfort versus style hadn't been an issue.

Maybe if she partly undressed, that would be provocative enough. She experimented with unfastening the top button, then the top two buttons. At last she undid all the buttons. Well, that wasn't any good. Underneath that black silk was that stupid plain bra.

Aha. She could ditch the bra. With that in mind, she ducked into the bathroom and closed the door. Then she locked the door. She didn't want Alec coming in while she was in the process of modifying her outfit. Very uncool.

She made it back into the room in less than a minute and stuffed the dorky bra into her purse beside the panty hose. Now the mirror revealed a barefoot woman dressed in a black silk skirt, panties and a suit jacket half buttoned. When she moved, only bare skin and a hint of shadowy cleavage showed.

But her hair was too carefully combed. She mussed it up. Good. Posing in front of the mirror, she arched her back and tossed her head. Then she pursed her lips and lowered her lashes. Not bad. If she'd ever had the nerve to do that in front of the camera, she might not have been such a washout as an actor.

Alec wasn't even in the room yet and she was already coming into her own. She smiled seductively at the woman in the mirror and made a soft purring sound. She was going to be bad, very bad.

The door lock clicked.

She leaped back from the mirror and frantically smoothed her hair into place. Who did she think she was? Then she buttoned her suit jacket all the way up to her neck and scrambled for her shoes.

She had one on and was hopping around trying to get the second one in place when Alec opened the door, the doggie bag in one hand and a single red rose in the other. Had she really invited him to make love to her all afternoon? She couldn't imagine herself ever doing such a thing!

Yet here he was, and she'd practically promised him that a fancy hotel room and her fantasy guy would make her lose her inhibitions. She'd hinted that if he peeled away her nice-girl persona, he'd uncover a purring sex kitten. What had she been thinking?

The room began to spin. Still holding her other shoe, she staggered back toward the bed and sagged against it while she struggled to breathe.

"Molly?"

"Oh, Alec. I...I think I'm going to faint."

4

ALEC KICKED the door shut and rushed over. Dropping the rose and the doggie bag to the floor, he lifted her onto the oversize mattress. Her feet dangled above the carpet. "Okay, now put your head between your knees." He guided her head down. Her hair was even silkier than he'd imagined, but he couldn't think about that now. His first priority was keeping her conscious. "Breathe deep."

She gasped for air.

"Through your nose. It gets the oxygen to your brain."

"How do...you...know that?"

"I was premed for a couple of semesters." He listened to her breathing and was relieved when it evened out. "It's okay. You'll be fine."

"I—I know. But I can't...believe this." Her shoulders started to shake.

"Molly, don't cry." He stroked her silky hair. "Everybody panics once in a while. It's nothing to be ashamed of."

"I'm not crying." Her giggles erupted as she lifted her head to look at him.

"Hey, you're not getting hysterical, are you?"

"Maybe." She grinned at him.

"I'll bet you could use some water." He started to turn toward the bathroom.

She put a hand on his arm, holding him in place. "That's okay. I'm fine."

"You're sure?" He peered into her face.

"It's just that..." She started laughing again.

"What?"

"Well, I didn't expect to end up with *my* head between my knees."

A rushing sound filled his ears and his heart started beating crazily.

She smiled at him, her pink lips parted, her cheeks flushed. "I thought most likely it would be *your*—"

He groaned and swooped in for the kiss, going from zero to sixty in three seconds flat, all his careful plans left in the dust. At last he was kissing Molly, and life couldn't be better. Her mouth tasted like cherry wine— sweet, rich, addictive. He wanted her naked and on her back in that bed. Now.

She seemed to be of the same mind. Shoving her fingers through his hair, she let him have his way with her mouth, and any woman that free with her mouth was ready for some serious loving.

He was just the guy to give it to her, too. Vaguely he remembered a different plan, one that didn't involve stripping her clothes off immediately, but nothing seemed more important than getting her out of her little suit. If only he could make some headway with the buttons on her jacket, they'd be in business.

Except he was at an awkward angle and the buttons were square. Whoever had put square buttons on this jacket should be shot. Then she got into the act, trying to help him. In the frenzied tangle of fingers, a button popped off and fell to the floor.

He drew back immediately, feeling clumsy. "Damn, Molly. I didn't mean to—"

"Who cares?" Breathing hard, she glanced down at the front of her jacket and fumbled with the buttons, managing to unfasten two more. "What idiot would think square buttons were a good idea?"

"Somebody who doesn't like sex."

"Exactly." She finally pushed the last button through the hole and glanced up in triumph. "There!"

As the lapels of the jacket drifted aside, Alec expected to see some kind of lacy bra appear. It took him a couple of seconds to realize it wasn't there. She was all creamy skin and tempting shadows just beyond the line of fabric. He gulped. "You aren't wearing a—"

"Nope." She braced her hands on the bed and gazed at him, her color high.

Desire tensed his muscles and interfered with his breathing. "You've been like that...all day?"

She smiled at him. "What do you think?"

He wasn't having much luck thinking about anything except what was under that jacket. "I think you're incredible. And full of surprises."

"Thank you." Her green eyes glowed. "And in case you're interested, the jacket's unbuttoned now," she added softly.

His voice was thick with anticipation. "Oh, I'm interested." He trembled as he imagined sliding his hands beneath the jacket. Then he remembered the rose he'd brought and then dropped on the floor when she'd started to faint.

It was now or never for that rose. He'd meant to hand it to her with a James Bond flourish, but that moment was long gone. Gazing at her open jacket, he could feel an even better moment coming up.

"I, ah, brought you a rose." He reached down and picked it up off the carpet.

"That's very sweet." She reached for it.

"Wait. Stay like that. Like you were before."

Looking puzzled, she braced her hands on the bed again. "Like this?"

"Like that. And let me...seduce you. Just a little."

A LITTLE WAS ALL it would take. Molly's nerves still vibrated from that humdinger of a kiss. She was ready to start removing clothes and testing the mattress. But if they plunged right in, so to speak, this encounter might turn out like the others she'd had—brief, mildly satisfying, ultimately forgettable. She didn't want that. She wanted to be inspired.

Alec himself was pretty inspiring, standing in front of her with a fragrant, blood-red rose in one hand. The bud was beginning to open, its outer petals gently unfurling, its inner ones wound into a knot of color. She felt like that rose, her center curled tight with promise while a sweet ache urged her toward the heat, toward bursting into bloom.

Alec's dark gaze swept over her and his breathing quickened. She waited, her heart dancing, to see what he'd do next. First, he brushed the velvety rose against her cheek, and the look in his eyes made her dizzy all over again. Remembering what he'd said, she breathed in through her nose, imprinting the scent forever on her memory. Now she would always think of Alec whenever she smelled a rose.

He dragged the rose gently across her lips, still moist from his kiss. "You have...a perfect mouth," he murmured.

Warmth crept through her, coaxing her into a lazy, sensual pace so different from the urgency of a moment ago. The muted sounds of traffic, buffered by the drapes, increased her sense of delicious isolation. Cocooned here with Alec, she could imagine herself doing...anything.

When she spoke, her voice was low and sultry. "Perfect for what?"

His breath caught. "For...for kissing...."

She dared still more. After all, no one would ever know. She swept a glance over his bulging fly. "And what else?" she asked softly.

His eyes darkened to jet black. "Oh, Molly."

"Did you think..." She paused as the image of slowly unfastening his fly took hold. She could almost hear the rasp of the zipper, feel the soft cotton stretched tight over his straining penis. "Did you think you would be the only one doing the seducing?"

The rose trembled in his grip and fell unnoticed to her lap. "Uh..."

"Because I expect this to be—" she hesitated on purpose, testing her power as she ran her tongue over her lips "—a two-way street."

His hot gaze still on her mouth, his expression one of a man who'd run smack into a door, he slowly nodded.

She had him. All she'd had to do was hint at oral sex, and he was totally hers. This was so brand-new, the burst of sexual courage that had allowed her to say such things. She'd never spoken that way to a man in her life.

But her first stab at talking sexy seemed to have immobilized him, and she didn't want that. He'd started something with the rose, and she wanted to find out how he'd finish it. She moved her hands back a fraction on the mattress, which allowed her jacket to slide open a little more. "You can go first, though."

He swallowed. "You...you're tying me up in knots here."

"Now *there's* an idea."

"*Molly.*" His expression tensed and his pupils dilated.

"Okay. I'll be quiet. But I didn't know talking sexy could be so much fun."

A muscle in his jaw twitched. "Keep it up and I'll be finished before I ever get started."

She was more powerful medicine than she'd thought. "You mean, if I keep making suggestive remarks, you would just..."

"Uh-huh. Sure would. I'm not far away from that point right now."

Thinking of him being close to that point stirred her up quite a bit, too. But she didn't want such a lovely reaction to be wasted. "That wouldn't be good."

"No."

"What did you have planned for the rose?"

He glanced at the flower in her lap with some surprise, as if he'd forgotten all about it. "I was...I was going to stroke you with it."

Her body tightened in anticipation. "That sounds nice. Show me."

He lifted the rose by the stem and touched it lightly against her throat. "Well, after I brushed it over your mouth—"

"Which is where we got sidetracked talking about—"

"Watch it."

She took a deep breath and forced herself to be quiet. Temptation was so hard to resist, now that she'd discovered he was so easy.

"Then I was going to slide it from here, all the way down to here." He trailed the rose slowly from her throat to the waistband of her skirt.

The petals slid lightly over her heated skin and it was *very* nice. She shivered in delight.

"Do you like that?"

"I do." Her breathing grew shallow. "What next?"

"This." He started at her collarbone and traced a path downward again, slipping the rose under her jacket so it caressed the swell of her breast. He hadn't touched her nipple, but it grew rigid anyway as a jolt of arousal shot down between her legs.

"And this," he whispered, starting at her collarbone again and drawing the plump cluster of petals under her jacket and directly over her nipple. But instead of continuing, he lingered there, brushing the petals back and forth.

She moaned and closed her eyes as control of the seduction shifted dramatically in his favor. She was so absorbed in the sensation of the rose softly massaging her aching nipple that she didn't know he'd eased aside her jacket until the velvet petals of the rose gave way to the slick heat of his mouth. The contrast was electric, making her gasp.

When she started to lose her balance, she discovered his arm circling her back, guiding her down to the mattress. He followed her there, spreading the jacket open with his free hand. Tenderness became lusty enjoyment as he took what he wanted without hesitation.

She arched upward, loving the possessive feel of his hands, his tongue, his teeth on her breasts. Her mind switched off as pleasure overrode every thought, every inhibition that had held her back before. She writhed beneath him, unabashedly taking all that he offered.

And then he drew back, leaving her damp and panting for more. She opened her eyes and found him propped on one elbow, simply looking at her. Her tongue was thick and unwieldy, but at last she managed to speak his name.

He glanced into her eyes, his expression taut, focused, hungry. "I had to see." Struggling for breath as he talked, he began to fondle her again, cupping and stroking each breast, feeding the fire.

"I wanted to see you lying there on the bed, your jacket open, your breasts bare and quivering, your skirt pushed up past your thighs."

Desire rocketed through her as his gaze traveled her body. And all the while he continued to knead her breasts and massage her nipples. She felt the beginnings of an orgasm, still deep inside, but rising quickly to the surface.

"I wanted to watch you arch your back and lift up toward me, asking for my mouth. I wanted to see how you look, all damp and pink where I've been licking you. I wanted to know the exact color of your nipples, and see how they pucker when you're hot."

She whimpered, nearly as turned on by what he was saying as by what he was doing to her.

"And you are so hot. The heat's coming off you in waves. The scent of aroused woman is filling this room. Your panties are already soaked, aren't they?"

Her reply was breathless, telltale. "Maybe." Her blood pumped through her at breakneck speed. And she knew what she wanted next, just in case he didn't. Speaking took great effort, but she managed to choke out the words. "Why...why don't you find out?"

His gaze intensified. "You know I'll make you come if I touch you there."

"Oh, I hope so." She took in his fierce expression. "But what about you? Is that putting too much of a strain on—"

"I won't come." His smile was grim. "As long as you keep your mouth shut."

Bold suggestions were so easy to make while she was hidden away with him in this hotel room. "I can't talk while you're kissing me, you know."

"Now *there's* an idea." He leaned over her, his eyes flashing dark fire. "God, I love your mouth." Then he proceeded to show her how much, kissing her so thoroughly that she almost missed his hand sliding up her skirt. Almost.

While his tongue thrust deep into her mouth, he drew a spiral pattern on her thigh, climbing higher with each rotation of his fingers. She forgot to breathe as he edged closer to the elastic leg opening of her panties. Almost there. The anticipation alone was threatening to give her an orgasm.

Slow gave way to swift and sure as he reached up and pulled her panties down. She gasped as he quickly probed her with nimble fingers. Two quick strokes and she arched off the bed, her cry of release muffled by the pressure of his lips against hers.

He lifted his mouth away as he finished the job with a steady rhythm that left her quivering and gulping for air. "I had to speed things up," he murmured, breathing hard. "I'm about to explode."

She was short on air and even shorter on working brain cells, but sexual craving was still high on her list. Despite that most excellent climax, she still wanted his penis buried inside her. Fingers were all well and good in an emergency, but she wanted the real deal. "Get...a condom," she said, panting. "Do me, Alec. Do me now."

He didn't have to be asked twice. The mattress bounced as he left the bed, and the sound of rustling plastic and ripping foil told her he was in as big a hurry as she was. Both hands went up under her skirt this time as he wrenched the wet panties down. They tickled against her ankle, dangling there as he shoved her skirt up to her waist and cupped her bottom in both hands.

"Wrap your legs around me."

She did, gladly. With one firm thrust and a deep groan of satisfaction, he introduced her to heaven. She was filled to the brim, and she loved it. As for that firm thrust, it was everything she'd imagined and more. Alec knew how to make an entrance, all right.

"Don't move a muscle." His voice was strained, his body rigid and his eyes glassy as he stood above her. "Let's see how long we can hang on."

She wanted to stay like this for a little while, too, so she tried to keep herself from welcoming him too warmly. That wasn't easy. She'd never invited such a well-endowed guest inside, and her entertainment committee was ready to start the party.

What a fantasy moment. This certainly wasn't the way a cautious, introverted woman ended up, with her jacket undone, her breasts exposed, her skirt bunched around her waist and her bare-bottomed chauffeur between her spread thighs, his large penis buried deep inside her. She even liked that Alec was still wearing his car service shirt with the logo on the pocket.

Mission accomplished. She was officially a naughty girl.

Alec moaned softly. "I can't believe how beautiful you look."

"You, too."

"Men aren't—"

"Yes, they are." Her heartbeat quickened as his fingers flexed, unconsciously kneading her bottom. "You should see the expression on your face," she said. "Like you're lit up inside."

He swallowed. "I feel like I am. Like I'm a... rechargeable battery...hooked up to the power source." He shifted his weight ever so slightly. "Ah, Molly."

He filled her so completely that she felt that tiny shift, and she quivered, balanced on the edge of ecstasy. She ran a tongue over her dry lips. "Interesting... comparison. About the battery."

"I was in—" He closed his eyes and clenched his jaw for a couple of seconds. "I was in electrical... engineering for a while."

"I believe it." She drew in a breath as he shifted his weight again. "I'm feeling very...electrified."

"Me, too." He opened his eyes again. Then he groaned. "Molly, I can't wait. I have to—" With a soft cry he clutched her bottom and started pumping, his breath coming in ragged gasps. "Oh, yes...yes...*yes.*"

She grabbed the bedspread and held on. That beautiful equipment of his brought friction to all the right spots, and soon she was spiraling out of control right along with him. As pleasure vibrated from the roots of her hair to the tips of her toes, she called to him, urging him on, asking for faster, harder, deeper.

He responded. Oh, Lord, how he responded. She'd never been stroked so hard and so fast, and never with such a magnificent instrument. She erupted while shouting his praises, and he followed right after, shuddering against her as he bellowed with satisfaction. Fighting for breath, he slipped his hands from beneath her, braced them on the mattress and slumped against the edge of the bed.

She didn't know how long she lay there still connected to him, his breath warm on her face, her eyes closed and a satisfied smile on her lips. Outstanding. Even after climaxing, he was still big enough to make her feel totally occupied.

"That...that was..."

Her smile widened, but she kept her eyes closed, still reveling in the picture of him driving into her. "Unbelievable."

"Mmm." He leaned down and kissed her smiling lips. "Gotta disappear for a minute. Don't go away."

"Wouldn't dream of it."

"Let's get you a little more stable. You're cantilevered out a little too far for my comfort."

She opened her eyes as he slid his hands under her. "Cantilevered?"

"Architecture. Four semesters."

"Oh." He had more facets than a Tiffany diamond, this chauffeur of hers.

"Up you go." He lifted her onto the mattress and ended their connection at the same time.

As he withdrew, she couldn't help making a little sound of disappointment. He felt so damn good in there. "Come back anytime."

"I'd love to." Then he nudged off his shoes, stepped out of his pants and walked into the bathroom.

As she listened to the water running, she sprawled on the satin bedspread, all sense of modesty destroyed. She wondered if it had been destroyed for good, or only for this afternoon, if she'd learned how to let herself go sexually in any circumstance, or only with Alec.

Lifting the foot where her panties still hung around her ankle, she kicked them into the air and caught them. She should probably get out of her jacket and skirt, too.

The skirt might be a lost cause, though, even if she took it off now. Her jacket was missing a button. An hour ago she'd been worried about the condition of her clothes when she left the hotel. Now she didn't really care.

Alec had helped her accomplish so much already. By the time they left this hotel room she might be a certified wild woman. She wondered what a certified wild woman would do while Alec was in the bathroom.

Get naked, most likely. Sitting up, she took off her jacket and tossed it on the nightstand. Then she flopped back down and shoved the covers to the foot of the bed with her feet. She'd started to shimmy out of her skirt when Alec came back.

"Hey, not so fast," he said, laughter in his voice.

She turned to see that he'd ditched the shirt. Apparently he'd decided to get naked, too, and she was so glad he had. Her first view of Alec without a shirt would go down in history, or at least her personal history. His manly pecs were decorated with downy hair and punctuated with nipples the color of milk chocolate. She wondered if she would have taken note of that if he hadn't been so eager to look at her. Sensuality was catching.

His waist and hips were slim, which she'd known. And now that she'd experienced his penis up close and personal, she knew it was the jumbo model. Even so, her eyes widened at the sight of it, still partially aroused, nestled against a backdrop of dark-brown hair and an impressive set of family jewels. His thighs were—

"Finished?" he asked softly.

"Not nearly." She remembered that she'd been about to take off her skirt, though, and he'd stopped her.

She'd forgotten the skirt, had almost forgotten to breathe during her intense study of his body. "Don't you want me to take off this skirt?"

"Sure I do. But with all that wiggling going on, you could have the decency to wait until I can watch."

"Oh." Her breasts tingled under his warm gaze. Well, of course she should let him watch. Obviously she still had a few things to learn about being a wild woman. "All right. I think I'll take off my skirt now."

"Okay."

She proceeded to take off her skirt an inch at a time, making sure her breasts shimmied with every movement. And each time they did, his penis twitched. "Enjoying this?" she asked.

"Obviously."

"Tell you what." She wiggled again, nearly free of the skirt now.

"What?" He was almost fully erect, and it was an impressive sight.

"When I finish this little chore, there might be something else I can do for you."

He drew in a breath. "Such as?"

"I seem to remember you saying I had a perfect mouth." Slowly she ran her tongue over her lips. "What do you say we take it for a test drive?"

5

MOLLY MIGHT NOT BE an X-rated movie star, but Alec felt as if he'd landed on the set for one of those flicks. His sexual history had contained a fair amount of excitement, but nothing to equal this—an expensive hotel room with a gorgeous redhead lying naked in the middle of a four-poster. And the redhead had just offered to give him a blow job.

Her green eyes sparkled, and she actually crooked a finger in his direction, beckoning him forward. He walked toward the bed, drawn there as steadily as if she had a fishing line attached to that finger and was slowly reeling him in. He also knew exactly which part of him she'd snagged, the part that was proudly leading the way, eager for the attention of her plump, pink mouth.

No woman had ever announced her intentions like this. Sure, he'd had women go down on him before, but it had just happened in the course of making out. Come to think of it, dialogue in general hadn't been a part of his sexual life. He hadn't realized how much it would turn him on.

"Where do you want me?" He sounded as if he had laryngitis. So much for Mr. Smooth.

She scooted over to make room for him. "Stretched out on this big ol' bed."

He had a sudden image of being tied hand and foot to the posts rising like phallic symbols at the corners of the bed. Damn, was he kinky? It was beginning to look that way. "Just, um, lying there?"

Her eyes widened briefly, and then a slow smile curved that mouth that would soon send him over the moon. "Maybe not."

Then again, he might not be ready for such doings. The idea sounded sexy in theory, but in reality, he'd be helpless. He wasn't sure if he could take that. "Just lying there is good," he said. "Just lying there is a wonderful idea."

"C'mon, Alec." Her cheeks grew pinker. "Do you have a four-poster at home?"

"No."

"Me neither. I've never had sex in a four-poster before."

"That doesn't mean we have to—"

"But why waste those wonderful posts?"

"You don't have anything to use for ties, anyway." He noticed the gleam in her eyes. "Do you?"

"I might. Lie down." She slipped off the other side of the high mattress, landing on her feet with a little thump. "And stretch out."

He eased down on the bed, more nervous than ever. Yet the forbidden thrill of what she might do next had made his penis stiff as a tailpipe. His brain might be trying to hold him back, but his libido was pulling him straight toward the flames.

From the bed he couldn't see what she was doing, but he could hear her rummaging through her purse. Then came the sound of shredding nylon. *Panty hose.* She hadn't been wearing them when he'd come up to the room, but she'd had them on earlier. He'd noticed their sheen as he'd helped her get in and out of the car.

Okay, panty hose ripped in half would only work to

tie his hands, so this would be Bondage Lite. He could deal with that. He wouldn't be totally immobilized, and he could—

She appeared at the edge of the bed with her panty hose, her purse strap and his belt.

He gulped. Then again, this could be the whole enchilada. He began to sweat, but his penis—well, his penis loved the entire kinky scene, apparently, because it was stretched to the max.

"Ready?" she murmured. "You look ready."

"I don't know about this." He eyed the equipment she clutched in both hands.

"First time?"

He hated to come off as unsophisticated. "Well, I wouldn't say that, exactly. I mean, I've had a few occasions when..." He paused and sighed. "Yeah, first time."

"Me, too." She was trembling. "What if I promise we can switch later? Would that help?"

Oh, yeah. Visualizing her staked to the four corners of this bed sent his pulse into overdrive. "Definitely."

"Then that's the deal. My turn first, then yours." She gazed into his eyes. "Okay?"

He trembled, still afraid he was in over his head.

She dampened her bottom lip with her tongue. He didn't know if she'd done it by accident or on purpose to remind him of what she'd promised to do once he was tied to the bed. In any case, looking at her glistening lower lip, so pouty and full, sent him over the edge into freefall. "Okay."

She took a shaky breath. *"Okay."* She surveyed the situation. "I think you should be in the middle of the bed."

Now that he was committed, he discovered that surrender could be very, very exciting. "You're the boss."

"Yes. Yes, I am." Her tone firmed up. "Move to the middle of the bed."

He scooted over.

She piled her stuff on the mattress beside him and pulled out a section of the panty hose. "Give me your wrist."

He held out his left hand.

She frowned in concentration as she tied the soft leg of the panty hose around his wrist and eased his arm up over his head to fasten the nylon to the bedpost. For a woman who claimed never to have done this before, she seemed to be a good hand at tying him up.

"Were you a Girl Scout?"

"No." She picked up her little pile of bondage equipment and moved to his left foot. "But I know how to sail, and sailors have to learn to tie knots."

He'd always wanted to learn to sail, but boats were expensive to rent and time had always been at a premium. He had a pretty good idea that money hadn't been a problem in her life. "In L.A.?"

"Uh-huh."

He could imagine her sailing around with some rich L.A. dude. He could imagine it, and he didn't like it one damn bit. The smooth leather of his belt caressed his ankle. Well, she was in New York City now. With him.

She slipped the belt off again. "This isn't working," she muttered. "Hold on a minute."

"You could forget my feet." He liked that idea. He wouldn't feel nearly as much like meat on the hoof if she only tied his hands.

"No. If we're going to do this, we're going to do it right." She padded back over to her purse.

"Molly, nobody would ever know if we did it right or not. That's the point."

"We would know. And we wouldn't get the full effect, either." She returned and circled his ankle with something white made of soft cotton.

He lifted his head to get a better look.

"Don't look."

"Why not?" He stared at his left foot. "You're tying me up with your bra?"

"It's a very boring bra." She cinched him to the bedpost with it and grabbed her last two restraints as she headed around the end of the bed.

"Anything you wear on those amazing breasts could never in a million years be classified as boring. An obstacle, for sure, but never boring." Talking made him forget that she was getting closer to having him totally in her control. "I'll bet it looks sexy on."

"It doesn't." She wound her purse strap around his other ankle and clicked the two metal fasteners together behind the third bedpost. "It's comfortable, but it makes me look like a frump."

"Frumps don't have breasts like yours, Molly." His chest tightened as she moved to the fourth bedpost. He'd never felt so vulnerable...and so turned on, in his life. His reaction to her was on full display, no place to hide. In a moment she'd be able to do anything she wanted with him, and however he responded would be right out there.

She grasped his wrist and her breath caught. "Your pulse is off the charts."

He turned his head to look at her. "Wait'll your turn comes. You'll understand."

She hesitated, the panty hose looped around his wrist. "Are you excited or nervous?"

"Both."

Uncertainty flashed in her eyes. "I can still stop. I could untie you."

He looked into those gorgeous eyes and damned if he wanted to be seen as a coward. He cleared his throat. "Like you said, we might not have another shot at a four-poster anytime soon."

Her lips were parted, her breathing shallow and quick. "That's what I'm saying."

It was skydiving time again. "Then do it. Have your way with me."

"All right, I will." She cinched up the panty hose and climbed onto the mattress beside him.

"Kiss me first." A kiss would personalize this. He didn't want to be treated like an object, a toy for her amusement. He wanted her to remember it was his cock she was teasing.

"I'd like that." Kneeling beside him, she leaned down, her hair falling against his cheeks as she lightly touched her mouth to his.

Instinctively he tried to cup her head with his hands, but the ties brought him up short. Instead, he had to lie there and let her decide how the kiss would go. His first taste of bondage, and he was already squirming, wanting to participate more than his restraints allowed. He lifted his head, trying to increase the pressure of the kiss, and she drew back, smiling.

"Lie down," she said. "I'm doing the kissing here."

With a groan he let his head fall back to the pillow.

"You're used to being in charge." She leaned forward again and nibbled at his mouth. "But this is about letting me be in charge. I get to have all the ideas, and you have to be the willing recipient of whatever I choose to give you." She outlined his lips with her tongue.

His chest heaved with each breath. This was going to be hell...and heaven. "Can I ask for stuff?" He wasn't in the habit of doing that, but then he wasn't in the habit of being tied up, either.

"Yes." She caught his bottom lip between her teeth and let it go. "You can even beg for stuff, if you want. In fact, I think eventually you won't be able to help it."

He thought eventually would arrive very soon. His penis ached something fierce, and he wanted her to at least touch it. "Grab hold of me, then," he murmured.

She laughed and rubbed her mouth back and forth over his. "That sounded like a command. Do you know how to ask nicely?"

"*Please* take hold of my cock, Miss Molly."

"In a minute."

He groaned again. "I'm in agony, here."

"Hate this, do you?" She licked the hollow of his throat.

"Not hate." The wet lap of her tongue taunted him with where else she could put it to use. He clenched his jaw. "I'm running a self-control deficit, though."

"A deficit?" She ran her tongue along his collarbone. "You sound like my tax guy."

"One semester of accounting."

"You're quite the Renaissance man." She used her tongue on his nipple but kept her hands braced on either side of him.

"Molly." He heard the desperation in his voice and didn't care. "Please touch me down there. Please do it."

"In a minute." She caught his other nipple between her teeth.

He'd had no clue what anticipation could do to a man. She was so close, yet so far. Her nipples brushed his ribs as she moved slightly lower. His penis quivered. He closed his hands into fists and tugged at the restraints, because the pressure might keep him from embarrassing himself by coming before she ever touched him.

When she dipped her tongue into his navel, he thought his trial would soon be over. He should have known better. Instead, she scooted down to his feet and ran her tongue over his instep.

He began to pant. "Just...wrap your fingers around my cock...one time. Just once, *please*." Then if he came, at least he could say it was because of some sort of hands-on attention.

"In a minute." She settled between his outstretched legs and licked the inside of his knees. Then she moved slowly up his thighs.

By this time he was gasping for breath and twisting against the restraints. "Molly...now...Molly...I need—"

"This?" She circled his penis with cool fingers.

He moaned and gritted his teeth. She was finally there, but he would not come yet. Would not. He wanted her mouth first.

She tightened her grip at the base of his shaft, and that helped. Then she began to tongue the tip, and that didn't help at all. When she began a slow massage of his balls, he started whimpering. It wasn't macho, but he couldn't stop the sounds any more than he could stop the way his body writhed against the sheet.

After an eternity in which he totally lost his cool but managed to keep from coming, she finally slipped her mouth down over him and began to suck gently.

He drew in a breath through clenched teeth. This was it. This was—

She stopped and moved away.

He yelled in protest.

"Want more?"

He groaned and pulled at the restraints.

"Say it, Alec."

"More, damn it!"

"All right." She leaned over and drew him in again, the suction greater this time.

He strained upward, wanting it, wanting it more than anything in the world. *"Don't stop."*

But she did. He lay there unable to do anything but moan as she untied each restraint.

"Now," she murmured, moving back over him, bending down, her hair tickling his groin. "Enjoy."

She took as much as she could into her mouth, increased the pace, and thank the Lord, increased the pressure. With a cry of relief he came so spectacularly that he thought for a second his heart had stopped. But no, it was beating like a jungle drum as the spasms of his climax made his body jerk, and jerk again. Then he collapsed onto the mattress, only vaguely aware that she'd crawled up beside him and snuggled close, her cheek on his heaving chest.

He had no idea how long it was before he found the strength to put his arm around her. Another space of time passed before he could get his vocal cords to work.

"Wild," he murmured.

"Good," she whispered back.

"That, too." Then he closed his eyes and drifted in a haze of sensual satisfaction so complete he thought heaven couldn't be any better than this. On the far reaches of his consciousness a thought tickled. This was very good. Maybe too good. He shoved it away. When it came to sex, there was no such thing as too good.

MOLLY DECIDED to let Alec sleep a little. They could keep the room for the whole night if they wanted it and they could probably both use a break before they continued this adventure. And what an excellent adventure it was turning out to be, too. She, Molly Drake, had tied up her first man.

Good thing it had been Alec's first time to be tied up, too. If she hadn't done everything exactly by the book, he'd never know. That thought reminded her of *her* book, the poor rejected baby stuffed into her shoulder bag. She'd had to move it aside to get her panty hose and her bra, but she'd been too involved in her mission to think about the book then.

Now that Alec was dozing beside her and the distraction of all that wonderful sex was temporarily gone, she thought about those dismal moments in Benjamin's office and got depressed all over again. Maybe Benjamin didn't know what he was talking about. A writing critique was always so subjective. Any writing class she'd ever taken had said that.

Benjamin saw her as a mystery writer who didn't deal with sex in her books. Maybe he'd read this manuscript with the wrong set of expectations, and that's why he hadn't been able to see its merits. She needed to look at it again. If she still liked it, she might need a different agent instead of more sexual experience.

Not that this afternoon hadn't been an excellent idea. And she had Benjamin to thank for giving her the courage to proposition Alec. Without Benjamin's harsh critique, she would never have dared so much.

Well, the manuscript was here and Alec was asleep. She could read it right now and decide whether to go agent shopping tomorrow. Come to think of it, she might have been naive to think that Benjamin could view her as anything but Dana's ghostwriter.

He had a nice income from those books, so why should he encourage her to branch out and possibly give up the ghostwriting? He was a smart man. He could have figured out that was her ultimate goal.

Now Molly could hardly wait to get her hands on the manuscript again. It was probably tons better than Benjamin had said. He just didn't want her to rock the very profitable boat that contained her, Benjamin and Dana.

Easing away from Alec, Molly slid to the floor. Because she hadn't become a complete wild woman, she walked to the closet, took out the hotel robe hanging there and put it on before she pulled her manuscript out of her shoulder bag. Then she settled into a wing chair upholstered in a blue and white print.

First she looked at the title page and her choice of titles. Maybe *Affair in Manous* wasn't evocative enough. It sounded too much like one of her mysteries.

Maybe she should call it something sexier, like *Jungle Heat*. She grabbed the pen resting on the hotel notepad by the phone and jotted that down. Something with jungle in the title was hotter than using the name of a city some people might not have heard of. She wanted them to get an image of primitive urges...like the urges she'd had once she'd tied Alec to the bed.

She sat in the chair sucking on the end of the pen for a good five seconds before she realized what she was doing—daydreaming about oral sex with Alec and using the pen like some sort of adult pacifier. But she'd had such wicked fun, and his penis was gorgeous. She could still taste... Okay, enough! She had a book to read.

Putting the pen down, she set the title page on the table beside her and started with chapter 1. After ten minutes she stopped reading and leaned back against the chair with a sigh. She wanted to believe it was good, but she couldn't tell. Benjamin's critique kept running through her mind. Maybe he was right. Maybe it did read as if it had been written by an introverted, cautious mystery writer.

Damn it. She'd wanted Benjamin to be wrong, but she couldn't tell if he was or not. That first sex scene did seem a little...stilted. Maybe. Or not. She closed her eyes, remembering the words, the sounds, the sensations from this afternoon. Now *that* was hot.

"Molly?"

She opened her eyes to find the man himself standing in front of her, a towel knotted around his waist. She'd been so absorbed in her book troubles she hadn't heard him get out of bed, let alone realize he'd gone into the bathroom to find a towel.

Funny, but he'd felt the need to cover up, too. She wondered if this sexual adventure they were having was as much of an unusual walk on the wild side for him as for her. Interesting thought.

"What are you doing?" he asked.

She glanced down at the manuscript. She'd promised to tell him about the meeting with Benjamin on the way home, foolishly assuming she'd have good news. But the news hadn't been good. Revealing her insecurities about this book to Alec would be much harder than taking off her clothes.

She didn't have to give him a straight answer. She could pretend it was a project she'd been working on, be vague about it and stuff it back in her purse. Or she could tell him about the manuscript and Benjamin's reaction and put far more than she'd intended on the line.

Weighing her options, she gazed up at him. She'd invited him to have sex with her, to explore mutual fantasies for hours on end in this hotel room. Before they left this place he'd know things about her that no one else had even guessed at. Private things. Intimate things. Carnal things.

Telling him about this writing project and her fears about it shouldn't be so hard, compared to that. But it was.

6

THEN, IN AN INSTANT, she made her decision. "I wrote this book." She held up the stack of pages.

"You wrote a whole *book*?"

She smiled. Little did he know that she'd written several whole books for the glory of Dana's publishing career, but she couldn't tell him that. "Yep, a whole book. The meeting today was with my agent, to find out what he thought of it." She decided to get the hard part over with fast. "He didn't like it."

"Aw, Molly." Alec dropped to his knees and put his hands on her shoulders as he gazed earnestly into her eyes. "That's only one person's opinion. You shouldn't let one opinion bother you. I'll bet it's a great book."

His instantly supportive reaction brought a lump to her throat. She had to clear it away before she could speak. "I don't know if it's any good or not. Benjamin—"

"That's your agent?"

"Yes, and he—"

"He's screwed with your confidence, is what he's done. I think you need a new agent."

She laughed, ridiculously pleased by his loyalty, even if he didn't have the foggiest idea what he was talking about. "Then again, Benjamin could be right."

"I'll bet he's not." Alec massaged her shoulders

gently through the terry-cloth robe. "What's the book about?"

"Sex."

He blinked. "You mean, like a how-to?"

"No, like a very erotic novel."

"Oh, *really?*" His eyebrows lifted. "And Benjamin didn't like it? He's probably gay, then."

She pictured Benjamin's horror at such a statement and smiled. "No, he's not, although gay people like sexy books, too, you know." Her smiled faded. "He said..." She paused and forced herself to repeat the criticism. "He said it sounds as if the author doesn't have enough experience to write about sex."

Alec's eyes widened as the implication of that sank in. "Is that what this afternoon is all about?"

She hesitated, then decided he should know the truth. "I hope you're not upset, but yes, partly."

"I don't know if I'm upset or flattered. I'm still digesting the information."

"Please don't be upset. It started out as a reaction to what Benjamin said, but once you said yes, I realized how much I've wanted you, wanted this. For weeks. I'm glad Benjamin said what he did, if it means I finally had the courage to ask you." She touched his cheek. "I've enjoyed every second with you, Alec. While we were in bed together, I forgot all about the book and what Benjamin said. No matter what happens, I'll always be grateful for today."

"Me, too." He caught her hand against his cheek and turned his head to kiss her palm. "And I'm not upset. How could I be upset about having some of the best sex of my life?"

"Thank you."

"It's the truth. I'm even grateful to your crummy

agent, if he's the one who made you think of this." He looked into her eyes again. "But I refuse to believe your book is bad. Let me read it."

With her free hand, she clutched the pages to her chest. "Oh, I don't think that's—"

"Come on, Molly. I've been to college for a lot of years. I had to take English courses besides all the other stuff."

"Yeah, what about all the other stuff?" She bought time with a change of subject. "How many different majors have you had, anyway?"

"Um, maybe five. I don't think you can count zoology."

"Five. That must have been expensive."

He nodded. "And time-consuming."

"I would think so! Okay, let's see." She ticked them off on her fingers. "Premed, accounting, architecture, electrical engineering and now law. That's quite a list, Alec."

"Yeah, I could design you a house, although I'm still a little shaky on where to put the bearing walls."

She appreciated what she saw as his attempt to make her feel better about the manuscript critique. "Small matter."

"That's what I thought. I also might be able to wire it, if you're willing to go with two outlets and no major appliances."

"Sounds okay to me."

"Plus, I could certainly balance your checkbook better than most, and I might even be able to perform an emergency appendectomy."

"And then handle the lawsuit if you slip with the scalpel?"

"Eventually." He grinned. "And that's a promise. I really am going to become a lawyer."

"So this is the end of the search?"

His jaw firmed. "Yes. I'm thirty-one, and it's time to stop this flailing around and settle into something. Law is it."

"I think you'll make an awesome lawyer." She had no trouble picturing him in front of a jury. He could easily convince her of the merits of his case, any case.

"Thank you, but I think we got sidetracked. We were talking about your career as an author." He reached for the manuscript. "Let me read the book."

She held it out of reach. "Now? Wouldn't you rather do something else with your time?"

"I'm a fast reader. That's what happens when you spend most of your life as a student."

"Alec, this book is three hundred and eighty-four pages long."

"So I'll read a chapter or two. That will be enough for me to confirm that ol' Benny is full of it."

She gazed at him, knowing she desperately needed another opinion. "If I let you read a couple of chapters, will you promise to give me your honest reaction?"

"I promise."

This was so much scarier than asking him to go to bed with her. Heart pounding, she peeled the first two chapters from the stack of pages and handed them over.

He took them and leaned closer to kiss her. "Thanks for trusting me," he murmured.

"I always have," she said without thinking. But it was true. She'd trusted him to drive her places and not endanger her life, and she'd trusted him to take her to bed and not endanger her heart. Now that she thought about it, he might be the only person besides Benjamin she dared show this book to.

Alec settled into the other wingback chair, and despite her feeling of trust, Molly wanted the chapters back immediately. She couldn't let him read them, even if he was the most trustworthy person she knew. She couldn't allow herself to be that exposed.

"Alec, wait a minute. I've changed my mind."

He glanced up at her. "Too late. But I should mention that when I'm finished reading and we've talked about your book, it'll be your turn in the four-poster. Whether you need the extra experience or not."

She was immediately wet and achy. "Way to take my mind off you reading the manuscript, Alec."

He grinned. "Did I? Excellent. All I really meant to do was warn you, so you'd be ready."

"I already am." She held his gaze, willing him to toss the pages aside and get out of the chair.

"Then see that you stay that way." He winked and went back to his reading, but the towel draped over his lap rose gently.

At least she could take satisfaction in that.

ALEC HADN'T READ MUCH besides textbooks for the past ten years, so he looked forward to finding out what Molly had written. He'd never known an author before, not to mention an author who'd written a book with sex in it.

He envied her the freedom to do whatever she wanted, though. Maybe she had a trust fund to draw from so that all she had to do was sit in that little cottage and write. If he could do whatever he wanted without worrying about starting a career, he'd...

The answer that flashed into his mind surprised the

hell out of him. If he didn't have to worry about getting ahead in the world, he'd probably keep driving for the car service. His dad, determined that his son wouldn't be blue collar like him, would sure hate to hear that.

Well, his dad wouldn't have to hear it, because after all these years and expense, Alec was by-God going to make it in a lucrative profession. He could definitely see the advantages of becoming a lawyer, too. For once he'd be in the same league with women like Molly. Too bad he wasn't closer to graduating.

Couldn't be helped. And right now he needed to concentrate on Molly's book. She wrote well, so at first he was ready to tell her this Benjamin guy needed an intellectual tune-up. But then he came to the first sex scene.

It seemed...awkward. He couldn't picture a guy making those kinds of moves on a woman, and her reaction didn't seem real, either. The talking before the sex was okay, but no woman spoke in complete sentences while she was having a mind-blowing orgasm. Molly's heroine did. And so did her hero. They used perfect grammar.

Plus they were way too polite with each other. The guy asked before he did anything to the woman, and his questions didn't have enough four-letter words in them. Maybe nobody had ever talked dirty to Molly Drake.

He could. His penis twitched, making the pages in his lap rustle. Miss Molly definitely needed to do some more research, and he was the most willing research assistant she could ask for.

He set the pages on the table and glanced up. She was watching him, her expression anxious. "You're a good writer," he said.

Although he hadn't added the word *but*, she'd obviously picked up the qualification in his statement, because her expression didn't change. "What else?"

He stood. "Don't worry. I know we can fix it, Molly."

She groaned. "You didn't like the sex scenes, either?"

"They sounded a little too...formal."

Molly squeezed her eyes shut. "Damn it. That's not what I want. I want lusty and uninhibited."

"I know." He stepped closer. "So here's what we're going to do. You and I are going to pledge to be lusty and uninhibited with each other. Afterward, you can take notes. Or we could use a tape recorder. That might be even better, because—"

"Wait a minute." She stared at him, her cheeks pink. "I appreciate what you're saying, but in the first place, we don't have a tape recorder in this room, and in the second place..." She frowned. "I forget what was in second place. A *tape recorder?*" She blushed a brighter shade of pink. "Do you realize what you're suggesting?"

He took hold of the shawl collar of her bathrobe and drew her toward him. "I'm suggesting that you do some field research on this subject. Trust me, after ten years in college, I am the research king of the world. The fastest way for you to get your characters to act like real people in bed is to tape-record real people doing it. Or video! Maybe we should rent a—"

"A *camera?* Oh, now you're getting ridiculous! I can't imagine setting up a camera in my bedroom and then having sex in front of it." But the gleam in her eyes said different.

He leaned down and brushed a kiss over her mouth. "I think you're imagining it right now, and getting turned on."

"Am not."

"Are so." With a firm yank he pulled the lapels of her robe apart and gazed down at her nipples, erect as pencil erasers. He flicked them with a forefinger. "May the record show I've entered these into evidence."

She swallowed. "Maybe the idea of filming us excites me, but the reality would scare me to death."

"Why?" He stuck two fingers into the tie around her waist and undid it. The robe fell open all the way down to her feet. "You're beautiful. You'd look wonderful on tape."

"I'd be embarrassed!"

"Not if nobody sees it but you. The videos would be your property, and I wouldn't even get to look." He cupped her breasts in both hands. "Unless I could talk you into letting me watch, which I'll probably try to do." He caressed her nipples with his thumbs. "Think of what a resource you'd have, Molly. You'll be able to describe how we look, how we sound, what we say."

Her breathing grew ragged. "I could just...rent some porn."

"Not the same. Those things are scripted and they usually sound that way, too. This would be the real stuff instead of that *oo, baby, oo, baby* junk."

"But...what about..." She leaned into his hands and ran her tongue over her lips. "What about...your job? If anybody finds out that you're involved with me, then—"

"You let me worry about that." And he wasn't even slightly worried about it, either. This was a project worth breaking rules for. "Your writing's great. Once you get the sex sounding better, you'll have a best-seller."

She swayed, her skin growing dewy with excitement,

her eyes becoming unfocused and darkened with lust. "What about...your studies?"

"Let me worry about that, too. I'll find time to study." He'd go without sleep if necessary in order to make this research project a reality. The risks involved made it even better. He hadn't taken nearly enough risks in his life.

"Oh, Alec, I don't know."

"I do." He shoved the robe from her shoulders and picked her up. "It's settled. And right now we have a date with a four-poster. Too bad we don't have the camera or a tape recorder, but afterward we'll write down every detail we can remember."

She wrapped her arms around his neck and smiled a siren's smile. "You don't want to take notes during?"

"Can't." He kissed her and placed her in the middle of the bed. "I'll be too busy making you come."

FOR THE NEXT HALF-HOUR, Molly didn't have the time or the inclination to think about her book, Alec's reaction to it or his plan to improve her sex scenes. She discovered that Alec had a talent for using his tongue, and that she was, contrary to her prior belief, multiorgasmic. By the time Alec freed her from the restraints and entered her, she was delirious with pleasure and positive she didn't have another orgasm available. She was wrong.

They made the bedposts quiver and the room echo with their cries until they finally collapsed, slick and satisfied, against each other. When Alec left the bed a few moments later, Molly rolled to her stomach and closed her eyes. Amazing sex could make a girl sleepy.

"No you don't." Alec was back, kissing her awake. "Don't conk out on me now."

She gazed at him through heavy-lidded eyes. "I can't

go another round, no matter how much you try. At least not until I've rested up."

"I'm not asking you to." He propped two pillows against the headboard and leaned against them, the hotel notepad balanced on his bent knee. "Just tell me what you remember about what we just did."

"I climaxed until I couldn't see straight."

"That's good." He scribbled on the pad. "How did it feel?"

"Good. It felt good." She closed her eyes again. "'Night, 'night."

"*Felt good* is not descriptive enough." He shook her gently by the shoulder. "Come on. You're a writer. I need something better than that."

"My brain is like fried oatmeal right now, Alec. I can't think of descriptions."

"Hey, I like that." The sound of the pen scratching on paper drifted between them. "Fried oatmeal. By the way, can you fry oatmeal?"

"Yes. Then you put syrup on it. Can I go to sleep now?"

"Syrup. I'm making a side note about that. We haven't even talked about what things we might put on ourselves, things we could lick off."

In spite of herself, she started to tingle again. She'd always wanted to squirt whipped cream all over a guy's penis. It would make a great visual, too. It—wait a minute, was she really planning to go along with Alec's video idea? Probably not. She'd freeze up the minute the camera was on.

"Can you remember what I said to you when I was whispering things in your ear and teasing you with my fingers?"

The tingling between her legs grew stronger. "Yes."

"What?"

"You told me that you were going to..." She couldn't say it out loud. Flopping to her back, she reached over. "Give me the pen and paper."

"You're not going to tell me?"

"Nope. I'll write it down." She grabbed the pen and started writing down all the things he'd promised to do to her. Even writing them made her blush, and it got her hot, too.

"I think it would be good if you learned to say those things."

"Maybe I will, but not yet. At least I'm writing them." She handed the paper and pen back to him. "How's that?"

He studied the page. "Pretty close. Good memory."

She didn't think she'd ever forget his deep, throaty murmur as he described his plans for her while she was tied to the bed. She didn't really need to write it down, but if it made him happy, she'd do it. Then she noticed that reading her words was having an effect on him.

"Alec, you're getting hard."

"Yeah." He gazed down at her. "From reading what you wrote. If you'd put something like this in your book—"

"If I'd put something like that in, Benjamin would have had a heart attack." She couldn't help smiling.

"Bet he would have tried to sell it, though, even from his hospital bed."

"Maybe."

"Now we need to add what you said during the whole bondage episode."

"I said things?"

"Oh, yes, ma'am. You weren't quite as graphic as I was, but I'm hoping you'll learn to be. Let's see, at one time when I was fooling around with your other excellent parts, you threatened bodily harm if I didn't put my head down between your legs immediately. I want to be sure and write that down."

"I did no such thing as threaten you!"

Alec grinned. "Did so. And then there was a lot of moaning when I finally got there. Not many complete sentences, but lots of words like *harder, faster, don't stop*. Things like that. And you panted a lot, too."

"I remember being so close I thought I would scream, but I don't remember telling you what to do."

He smiled down at her. "Doubting my word?"

Considering the red haze that had settled over her brain from the moment he'd tied the last restraint and started touching her, she wouldn't swear that she hadn't said those things in the heat of the moment.

"Oh, and the third time, you yelled out, *'I'm coming! Again! Unbelievable!'*"

She squirmed against the sheet. It had been unbelievable, and what was more unbelievable, she wanted him again.

"See what a description of real sex can do?" he said softly, laying aside the pen and paper and sliding down beside her. "Make your readers feel like that, and I guarantee you'll sell your book."

She turned to her side and reached down to curl her fingers around his erection. "Right now, I don't care about the book."

"No? What do you care about?"

"Finding out where my next orgasm is coming from."

He smiled at her. "And what would you like me to do, Molly?"

She hesitated. Writing certain words was one thing, but she'd never had the nerve to actually say them.

"Let go. Say the words. If I can use them, so can you."

There was a first time for everything. As a budding wild woman, she could expect a lot of first times in her future. Heat poured through her as she leaned forward and whispered the two-word, explicit request in his ear.

He rolled her to her back and reached for another condom. "I'll be glad to."

7

BECAUSE ALEC KNEW THAT tonight wouldn't be the end of his time with Molly, he didn't mind so much when they finally agreed to leave the hotel. He had to admit that they should return the car before anybody happened to notice it was still out of the lot. Returning it at two in the morning when his boss knew he'd only meant to drive Molly into the city and home again wasn't a smart move.

Although keeping his job was now less important than having sex with Molly so she could write a better book—what a no-brainer that had been—he might as well try to keep his job *and* fool around with Molly. He wasn't very good at being devious, but he'd give it his best shot.

While he got dressed, Molly did an amazing job of resurrecting her silk suit. She reattached the button using a little sewing kit she found in the bathroom and then pressed both the jacket and skirt with the iron and ironing board stored in the closet. Leaving her alone to iron the outfit hadn't been easy when she looked so great standing there in her underwear.

There was not a single thing boring about her bra. Or maybe the white bra and panties looked even more provocative because they weren't meant to be. There was something innocent and schoolgirlish about the plain cotton, especially when he thought about what they'd used the bra for and the anticipation he'd felt pulling off those simple panties right before he plunged into her for the very first time. He needed to stop thinking about that before he walked over and pulled them down again.

Once they were both dressed, Molly used the video-checkout option so they wouldn't have to go back to the desk at this hour of the night. They could leave the hotel as if going out for a late snack and just not return. The idea that he might never see this particular room again bothered Alec, though. He'd had one of the most significant sexual encounters of his life here.

So he memorized the room number and slipped a wrapped bar of soap into his pocket when he thought Molly wasn't looking. They'd used the other bar when they'd taken a shower together and had ended up fooling around, of course. The bar of soap in his pocket would help bring back the memory of the water pelting them as they stroked each other to a shattering climax.

It was probably a good thing they were leaving. He'd amazed himself by getting it up five times tonight, but sooner or later he'd reach his limit and he wanted to quit while he was ahead, while Molly still thought of him as a stud.

"I guess that's it, then," Molly said.

"For this room, anyway." Alec didn't want any hint of finality slipping into this exit. "On to bigger and better things."

She moved closer to adjust the collar on his shirt. "I still think you're taking too much of a chance, Alec. If anybody finds out about us and you get fired...I'd never forgive myself."

"Nobody's going to find out." He loved having her

fiddle with his clothes the way an actual girlfriend would.

"I hope not, because—"

"Come here." He set down the plastic bag containing their leftover lunch and pulled her into his arms, shoulder bag and all, for a long, wet kiss that left them both breathing hard. "Now tell me again that you don't want me to help you with your sex scenes."

She took a shaky breath. "If you kiss me like that nonstop, or better yet, keep me in bed constantly, then I'll never worry about anything."

"There's a concept. Marathon sex until we both get it right. I'll bet that would give you plenty to write about."

"And you'd flunk out of law school *and* lose your job. No dice."

"Okay, no marathon. But I am going to work on this project with you. And it will be awesome, so you might as well go along with it and stop trying to buy trouble, as my mom would say."

"We'll see how it goes." Then she looked at the plastic bag on the floor at their feet. "We should probably eat that on the way home, huh?"

Alec looked at the bag they had decided to take with them from the coffee shop. After ten years of being a student, he was tempted to take it along, but the food would be awful by now, if not downright dangerous. Molly might be determined to eat it because he'd bought it for their lunch.

"Are you hungry?" he asked.

"A little."

He was suddenly starving, his stomach cramping with the need for food. She was probably in the same condition and didn't want to admit it. "We'll pick up a hamburger on the way home, like we planned." He walked over and dropped the bag in the wastebasket.

"Wait!" She started toward the wastebasket.

"Leave it." He caught her arm. "Let's go."

"But lunch was your treat, and here we are letting it go to—"

"I've had so many treats tonight, I can't count them all. Forget the wasted food. Besides, it might give us both food poisoning after sitting around unrefrigerated for so long. We couldn't videotape ourselves having sex if we're hurling, now, could we?"

She gazed at him, her cheeks pink. "Are you sure you really want to do that videotape thing?"

"Oh, yeah. And so do you. I can see it in those green eyes. You can hardly wait to try it."

Her breathing quickened. "I bet I'll chicken out at the last minute."

"Not if I can help it." He waggled his eyebrows at her. "And I think I can."

Her gaze became even hotter. "Let's go," she said, her voice throaty. "While we can still make it out the door."

"Good plan." He opened the door for her. Before he followed, he took one last look at the rumpled bed, the towels on the bathroom floor, the wastebasket that held several used condoms in addition to the doggie bag. Maybe, someday in the future, he'd bring Molly back here.

Or maybe not. By the time he became a lawyer and had some walking-around money in his wallet, she might have found somebody else. If she became a publishing success, she could definitely leave him in the dust. By helping her improve this book he could be giving her the ability to rocket right out of his life.

He closed the door. He would help her anyway, because he'd always been good at helping people, and because the sex was amazing, and because...because he cared about her more than was good for him.

Riding down in the elevator, they kept glancing at each other and smiling, two people with a secret.

"Do I look okay?" Molly asked as the lobby floor grew nearer.

"If you mean do you look as if you've spent the afternoon and evening romping in bed with me, I don't think so." He almost wished she did. He wouldn't mind having people know that for now, she was his girl. "If you mean how do you look in general, you look fantastic, as always."

"Thanks. You, too."

He glanced down at the car service logo shirt which still had a smudge from his tire-changing episode. "This is definitely high fashion, I'll give you that."

"You look like my boy toy."

He laughed. "I thought that when we first came into the hotel. Do you like that fantasy?"

"Uh-huh."

As he looked into her eyes, he started getting hard. He'd worried about his stamina, and yet here he was, aroused again. He cleared his throat. "You'd better wipe that expression off your face before we get to the lobby if you don't want anyone to guess what we've been up to, Miss Molly."

"You know, I've just decided I don't care what they think."

"Good. But there's another issue at stake. If you don't stop looking at me that way, I'm liable to drag you to one of those cushy sofas in the lobby and try to take your clothes off."

Her eyes widened. "You would?" She sounded more excited than shocked.

He blew out a breath. "Damn, Molly, but you're one hot woman. We'll be lucky to get all the way home without pulling onto a side road for a quickie."

"I thought of that, too!" she said, almost wailing. "Do you think I've turned into a nymphomaniac?"

Alec laughed and gave her a quick kiss full on the mouth. "I think you're loosening up for the first time in your life, and it feels so good you want to keep doing it. You'll probably settle down in a little while."

He needed to keep that in mind. He'd happened upon Molly right when she was ready to cut loose, which made him, the guy who was helping her, seem more important than he really was. This wasn't really about his abilities as a stud, or even her special feelings for him as a person. This was about Molly finally bursting into bloom. He was a means to an end, not an end itself. That depressing thought was enough to cool his jets for a while.

What he should do, he decided as they walked into the deserted lobby, was think of Molly in the same way. He'd never totally let himself go with a woman, either, which explained his constant state of arousal with Molly. No woman had ever asked him to be her fantasy man before. Molly could be a means to an end for him, too. By participating in her adventure, he'd kick off the traces himself. Together they'd escape the ordinary, and then go their separate ways with an expanded idea of their sexual potential.

Well, didn't that just sound like something out of one of his psychology textbooks? And it was a pile of crap. If he had glorious sex with Molly for whatever time they stayed together, he'd be hurt when she decided to end it. Guaranteed.

He glanced at her walking beside him through the lobby, the light reflecting off her red hair, her body moving with a fluid grace he hadn't noticed before. Fantastic sex looked good on her, and he wanted to hang around as long as he could. So he'd end up hurt. It would be worth it.

MOLLY DIDN'T REALLY THINK she was becoming a nympho, but she was a little unnerved by her response to Alec. She'd never had so much sex packed into a few short hours, and on the ride home, she wanted more. This incredible lust had the power to make her forget everything, including the risks Alec was taking with his job and his studies. Although he'd said that was his concern, she'd started this affair, so it was her responsibility, too. Wild-woman-training or not, she would keep some control over herself.

That was easier said than done, especially when they were cruising down the turnpike, each of them eating a juicy hamburger, and she turned to catch Alex biting into his. All she could think about was what he'd done to her after tying her to the bedposts. She was pretty sure some of those things were illegal in a few states. And she'd loved it all. She wanted more. Now.

Instead, she crossed her legs and squeezed her thighs together to soothe the ache. Alec needed to get the car back, and if they turned off to make out in the back seat, no telling how much longer this trip would take.

"You're quiet over there," Alec said. "Something wrong?"

"Nope."

"Thinking about sex?"

"I do have other topics to think about, you know."

"You were thinking about sex." He laughed and popped the last of his hamburger into his mouth.

"Not exclusively."

He chewed and swallowed before reaching for the soft drink sitting in his cup holder. "I have. I've been imagining what you'd look like naked on that leather back seat."

"Stop it, Alec. We are not going to park somewhere and have sex. That's final."

"Why not?"

"Because we completely forget about time when we do that, and we need to get this car back. You said so, yourself."

"Okay, so you'll only be seminaked. I'd just take off enough for a quickie, like I said earlier. Ever had one of those?"

"Not on purpose."

"Gotcha. Quickie for him, crummy for you. I won't let that happen."

She was quite sure he wouldn't. If he could give her two orgasms to his one, he'd do it. And once he was rolling, she wanted the pleasure to last forever. "You know what? I don't think we're capable of a quickie."

"Sure we are." He put the right-turn signal on and pulled into the exit lane.

"Alec! I didn't mean that as a challenge. Get back in the through lane." Her panties were already wet, just thinking about a quickie.

"Five minutes extra. Five minutes is nothing."

"You're flirting with getting yourself fired!"

"I'm flirting with you." He reached over and stroked a hand down her thigh. "This'll be really fast, I promise. While I'm finding a quiet little spot, you can take off your shoes and your panties. Oh, and I think we put the box of condoms in your purse, so if you'd—"

"You're crazy. Stark raving mad."

"And you need ideas for your writing." He turned right off the exit ramp and took another right down a two-lane road. "Take off your panties, Molly."

"I suppose if I don't, you'll talk me out of them, anyway."

"Yes, I will, but that'll take longer. If you're worried about time, you'd better do it."

So she did, nudging off her shoes and lifting up against the seat belt to work her panties down.

He took a deep breath. "Don't tell me you don't want to do this. You're drenched in eau de arousal."

"And it's freaking me out! I've never been like this."

"Neither have I, babe." He swerved into the parking area of a little roadside fruit stand, boarded up because the fruit season hadn't begun yet. He drove the car around behind the stand. "Perfect. Got the condom?"

She handed him the packet.

"Excellent." He flipped the automatic locks open. "Meet you in the back seat, you juicy woman, you."

She opened the door and the dome light came on. With a soft oath Alec hit the switch and they were in darkness again. She stepped out onto a carpet of new spring grass that tickled her bare feet. The air was chilly, but it smelled sweet all the same, like budding flowers.

The back door of the car on her side flipped open. "Hey, no time to stargaze," he said. "We have urgent business here."

Laughing, she climbed into the back seat. "Now this is romance at its finest."

"This is called sexual efficiency. The most bang for your buck."

"Very funny." As her eyes adjusted to the darkness, she could see him leaning against the far side of the car. He'd already unfastened his pants and he was rolling the condom over a very firm erection.

"How did you get so hard so fast?"

"That's what you do to me, Molly. Now be a good girl and come sit on my lap. I have something for you."

"So I see. Are you sure this is going to work?"

"We'll make it work. Pull up your skirt and come here."

She bunched her skirt around her waist, knowing it would get wrinkled again, but it didn't matter now because they had no lobby to walk through.

"Oh, Molly, how I love to see you with your skirt like that. Will you do that for the video?"

"I still don't think we'll be making that video."

"I do." He grasped her hips. "Now straddle me. The clock's ticking."

Balancing herself by holding on to his shoulders, she put her knee on the seat between his hip and the backrest, and her other foot on the floor.

"Mmm. Come to me, my Molly." He guided her to the right spot.

She caught her breath at his possessive words. They touched a secret yearning that had taken root, a desire to turn this into more than a temporary affair. Then nothing else mattered but the sensation of the blunt tip of his penis sliding unerringly inside. She should be used to the electric feeling of connection, but it still had the power to make her dizzy with urges she could barely control. Eyes closed, she eased down, taking him in.

"So good," he murmured, his fingers squeezing her bare bottom under the bunched skirt.

"We're depraved," she whispered back, gazing at him in the dim light.

His teeth flashed in a grin. "Yeah. Don't you love it?"

"I do." She wiggled against him.

"Oh, Molly."

"You wanted this to be quick, right?"

"Yes, but I made some promises, too. Hold still a second. I need to get set."

She wiggled again. "I don't think you could be any more set than you are, in the back of a luxury car with a willing woman astride your favorite body part."

"We need a tape recorder. That was cute."

"Forget the book. We need to get this done. I—" She moaned softly as he slipped his hand under the front of her skirt and rubbed his knuckle gently right where he knew she needed that extra pressure.

"Come," he murmured. "Come while you're perched right there, and I'll bet you'll bring me right with you."

The tightening began, coaxed by the steady rhythm of his knuckle. She gulped for air. "And if...I don't...take you with me?"

"I'll make you come again, and see if it works the second time."

She closed her eyes again. Instinct took over as she moved her hips in a tight, slow circle, never moving so much that she'd lose contact with his erotic touch.

"Oh, man." He started breathing faster. "Whatever you're doing there, swivel-hips, keep it up."

"Same...to...you." And with that she climaxed, crying out as she dug her fingers into his shoulders.

"Ahhh...yes...*yes!*" He thrust upward, driving into her as spasms shook him.

She leaned her forehead against his as they both struggled for breath. "So...that's your...idea of a quickie?"

"Uh-huh." He massaged her bottom and cleared his throat. "Like it?"

"It's okay."

"Just okay?" He pinched her lightly.

"Ooo!" She was amazed at the sharp thrill of that pinch. "I mean, ow!"

"Too late, lady. I heard the *oo*, and now I know you might like a little kinky pinching next time. How do you stand on love bites? That could be fun, too."

"Never mind!" She tried to move away from him. He was uncovering forbidden fantasies way too fast for her comfort.

He held her tight. "I think we should stay here a little longer. Things are just starting to get interesting."

"We are not staying here longer." She cupped his face in both hands. "Now let me go, and let's get this car back where it belongs. We can discuss that...other stuff later."

"Promise?"

She caressed his cheeks, which were starting to bristle with a growth of beard, and looked into his eyes. "Alec, where are you taking me?"

"Home, according to you."

"No, I mean—"

"I know what you mean," he said gently. "And I'm not taking you anywhere you don't want to go. And wherever I do take you, remember that I'll be right there with you. I'm exploring, too, and we'll go slow. There's nothing to be afraid of."

She gazed at him for a long time. *Except losing my heart.* "You're right. There's nothing to be afraid of."

8

ALEC TOOK MOLLY BACK to her cottage in Old Saybrook, even though she tried to talk him into dropping the car at the lot in New Haven and driving her home in his Blazer to save time. Although his boss, Nick Edgars, wouldn't be around at one in the morning, the surveillance cameras would be on. Alec could create a cover story for why he was so late returning the car in case Edgars asked. But he'd never be able to explain why a gorgeous redhead had climbed out of the vehicle and into his Blazer, in case Nick happened to review the tape.

He saw Molly to her front door and kissed her, of course. Then he had to tell her how wonderful the day had been, which led to more kissing while she told him how much their time together had meant to her. More kissing and fondling followed, and he would have stepped through that door with her if she hadn't gently pushed him away.

"Go home," she said softly as she opened the door. Then she turned back to him. "We both need sleep and you have to take the car to the lot."

He shoved his hands in his pockets so he wouldn't reach for her again. "I hate it when you're right."

"Good night, Alec."

"Wait!" He put a hand on the door before she could

close it. "We haven't set up a time to...um—" *to have sex again* "—to get together."

"Oh." She hesitated. "I guess that's up to you. You're the one with the heavy schedule."

"Tomorrow afternoon works."

"It does?" She frowned. "Isn't tomorrow Wednesday?"

Wednesday was already here, but he didn't bother to point that out. "Yes, why?"

"I thought you had class all day on Wednesday. That's why I made my appointment with Benjamin for Tuesday, because I knew you were usually free to drive."

He shrugged. "Normally I'm in class on Wednesday afternoons, but tomorrow is mostly review."

She eyed him suspiciously. "How convenient."

"Seriously! No big deal. I was thinking of skipping those two classes anyway. I have a driving gig at six tomorrow night, but my afternoon's free."

"Which means you could spend it studying, or doing research in the law library, or—"

"Or research in your bedroom." He held her gaze. "I'm a big boy. I can handle my class schedule. Now, if you've changed your mind about seeing me again, that's a different story." He held his breath, praying she hadn't.

"You know I want to see you again."

He sighed in relief.

"But I don't want to jeopardize your studies."

"You'll inspire my studies," he said. "I'll have a reason to do everything faster and better so I have more time to be with you."

"That had better be true."

"It will be. So, tomorrow afternoon about one?"

Her answer was a little breathless. "Um, sure."

He liked knowing he affected her that way. "Is there somewhere in town where you could rent video equipment, or do you want me to take care of that?" His groin tightened.

"You want it tomorrow?" She swallowed. "Maybe we should wait on that."

He didn't think so. They'd both lose their nerve. "Tell you what, I'll pick up a camera and tripod, and if you don't want to use it, that's okay."

"No." Her jaw firmed. "I'll get the camera, if anybody's going to. It's for my book."

"Yeah." He winked at her. "You can write it off on your taxes."

Her eyes widened. "No way."

"Loosen up, Miss Molly. No one will know whether you took pictures of the blossoms in springtime or writhing, naked bodies. Just make sure the tape can go straight to your TV. Once you've seen it you can destroy it."

"Oh. I guess you're right."

"Taping us is a good idea. I'll bet it really jump-starts those sex scenes of yours."

"I believe you. It's just that I—"

"Don't think about it in advance. Get the equipment and pretend you're going to use it to take pictures of the sunrise down on the beach." He leaned through the partly open door and gave her another swift kiss. "See you at one."

Then he hurried down her flagstone walk before she could create any more hurdles. He wondered if she'd rent the video equipment, or if he'd arrive tomorrow afternoon and discover she'd chickened out. Oh, well.

Camera or no camera, he could hardly wait to climb back in bed with Molly Drake.

Visions of making love to her in that dollhouse of a cottage carried him down the turnpike to New Haven in fine style. He'd fudged a little on the "mostly a review" evaluation of tomorrow's classes. But he had friends who would share notes with him.

Technically he had no leeway this week, so he'd have to cut some corners to spend a few precious hours with Molly. If he'd told her the truth about his packed schedule she wouldn't have agreed to any more time together until after finals. He wasn't about to let that many days go by.

The main consideration was her book. The sooner she wrote some believable, hot sex scenes, the sooner she'd realize her dream of publication. But if he didn't push this sexual-research project, she might start having second thoughts about it. Besides, if he didn't find ways to be with her, he'd go insane with unsatisfied lust. He'd be no good at school or at work, so in a way, he had no choice but to work her in as best he could and sacrifice a few other things.

Caught up in his thoughts about Molly, he was at Red Carpet's automatic security gate before he knew it. As he activated the rolling gate and pulled the Town Car inside, he noticed Josh sliding out of the driver's seat of a white stretch limo. Josh saw him and waved.

So he'd have to talk to Josh before he left, and he quickly thought about how much he wanted to say. He trusted Josh. He really did. After all, they'd been buddies since junior high, and Josh had put in the good word for him at Red Carpet.

Maybe it was all that history that made Alec worry about how much to reveal about his situation with

Molly. Josh had been riding him pretty hard about putting his brains to work and finally getting a degree in something. Josh might see the Molly complication as a threat to that goal.

By the time Alec had parked the Town Car in its assigned space and locked it, Josh was on his way over. Although it was past two in the morning, Josh had a spring in his step and a smile on his face. He wore the dressier uniform required when anyone took out the stretch limos, but he had the tie loosened and the cap turned backward now that he was off duty.

Josh had always been high-octane. His friends used to tell him that all that excess energy was what made his hair so curly. Alec had only seen him depressed once, and that was right after his dad died. But Josh had bounced back from that blow and now his Energizer Bunny routine was stronger than ever.

"Late night, college boy," Josh said. "Did Edgars send you on some last-minute gig?"

"No." Alec threw the keys in the air and caught them so he'd appear nonchalant. "On my way to Molly's this morning, I stopped to help this old couple change a tire, and so Molly was going to miss her train. I drove her into the city."

"Did you, now?" Josh's gray eyes missed nothing. "That must have been some trip."

"Uh, well, we—"

"I think that would be lipstick on your sleeve, old buddy."

Alec pulled his right sleeve closer so he could see what Josh was talking about. Nothing was there.

"Other sleeve," Josh said. "Which is what makes it so interesting. I can understand if she leaned over and accidentally tagged you on your right sleeve while you were driving. But the left sleeve, now, that has me speculating."

Alec didn't have to look at the other sleeve to remember exactly when Molly must have branded him. She'd redone her lipstick in the elevator on the way down to the lobby. No doubt that lipstick had ended up on his sleeve during the episode in the back seat of the Town Car.

In the dim light inside the car, neither of them had noticed it. He would have seen it in the glow from her porch light, but he'd been too intent on her. And she'd been too intent on the idea of that video.

"Is it safe to say you're breaking company rules?" Josh asked.

"It's probably better if I don't tell you anything about it. That way if Edgars ever finds out, you can truthfully say you didn't know what was going on." Nice dodge, if he did say so himself. He might make a decent lawyer, after all.

"You're kidding, right? I don't give a damn about Edgars. Is she a porn star or not?"

Then again, this was Josh he was dealing with. Dodges didn't work with Josh. "No. Definitely not."

"You're sure? Because I could swear she looks almost exactly like that one who made *Slippery When Wet*. She might not want to tell you, you know."

Alec thought about Molly's fears about making even a private video. "I can guarantee she's not the star of *Slippery When Wet*."

"Then what about all the trips to L.A.? What does she go out there all the time for, if she's not making X-rated flicks?"

"Well, she—" Alec realized that although he had some very special knowledge about Molly, specifically her response to certain sexual stimuli, he had no idea why she flew to L.A. a couple of times a month. Even if she went to visit her family, that was damn excessive for a grown woman to need so much mommy-and-daddy time.

"You don't know why, do you?" Josh asked.

"We didn't get into that, but I'm sure she has her reasons."

"Oh, I'm sure she does. Like maybe a steady boyfriend in California."

"That's not it!" Alec went rigid at the idea. Molly wasn't the kind of woman to use him for sex while she was in Connecticut and then fly back to some rich but sexually boring boyfriend. He couldn't believe that of her.

"From your reaction, I'd say you and Molly Drake got very friendly."

Alec didn't want to talk about that. "She's an author. I'm going to help her with her book."

"Her *book?*" Josh laughed. "And you'll be doing this when? Your schedule's so tight you barely have time to shave in the morning. In fact, I thought you planned to catch up on the reading for your family law class today. I'm assuming the books stayed in the trunk."

"Damn, thanks for reminding me." Alec walked over to the Town Car, unlocked the trunk and took out a stack of textbooks. He'd brew a pot of coffee when he got home and do some reading before his first class at eight.

"Alec, Alec, Alec." Josh shook his head. "I admit Molly's gorgeous, and I don't blame you for trying to get a little, but promise me you won't throw a semester of hard work out the window. Not again."

Nobody seemed to have faith in his ability to multi-task, Alec thought grumpily. "I won't."

"I don't know what kind of book she's writing, buddy-boy, but you so don't have the spare hours to help her. I hope you know that."

"Don't worry. I'll be fine."

"Yeah, sure, Sir Galahad. Here you go, riding to the rescue again, letting all your own stuff languish by the wayside. Listen, stick with this lawyer thing and one day you'll be pulling down three or four hundred grand a year, easy. No woman's worth sacrificing an opportunity like that."

Molly might be. "I don't intend to sacrifice myself."

"That's what you always say, and then you do it, anyway. Just this once, be like me. Look out for *numero uno.*"

"I do!" This was an old argument, and he got drawn into it every damn time.

"The hell you do. You're hopeless. First you stopped to help the old couple. Then you couldn't let Molly be late, so you offered to drive her into the city, taking extra time you don't have. Okay, so the hanky-panky is understandable, given that you've lived like a monk recently, but you certainly don't have to help her write some *book,* for crying out loud."

Alec decided not to explain that helping with the book would be as much his gain as Molly's. Any guy given the chance to "help" a woman like Molly with her sexual knowledge would jump at the idea. Even Josh. But Josh had his standard *if I had your brains* speech, and Alec had learned to let him finish.

"If I had your brains I'd go for the law degree," Josh said, "but I don't. That doesn't mean I don't have a plan. For your information I'm only a year or so away from starting my own car service."

"That's great, Josh. Really great."

"My point is, no woman is getting in the way of Josh Gregory's plan for advancement. I don't care how good she looks or how great she is in bed."

"I have to say you've stuck to your plan." But privately Alec thought that if Josh were tempted by the likes of a woman as sexy as Molly, he might not be quite so cocky. Alec had a sneaking suspicion that Josh hadn't met his match. At one time, Priscilla Adams had looked like a good candidate to knock Josh off his perch, but now Pris was marrying somebody else.

"And you need to stick to your plan for a change," Josh said.

"I promise to take everything you've said under advisement."

"See that? You already *sound* like a lawyer. All you need is the shingle, man, and you'll be golden. I plan to be your first client, before you get too expensive for me."

Alec laughed. "You're already figuring on breaking the law?"

"Hell, no. I want you to be ready to go over the contract when I buy my business, to make sure I'm not getting screwed."

"So you're saying that I should specialize in contract law."

Josh ignored the dig. "Doesn't matter. You'll still be able to sort through all that legal mumbo jumbo better than I ever could." He clapped Alec on the shoulder. "Is it a deal?"

"Sure. Anything for you, Josh." All the while they'd been talking, Alec had been thinking ahead, beyond tomorrow afternoon's date with Molly. "Listen, are you scheduled to drive Thursday night?"

"Not yet. So far I just have an airport run in the morning. Why?"

"Edgar has me down for that fortieth-birthday dinner thing. I wondered if you could take it."

Josh eyed him. "So you can study?"

"I'll study during the day. But I need—"

"I know exactly what you need, stud. And I can always use the extra income, but the thing is, so can you. Can you afford this woman?"

"I have savings."

"For next fall's tuition, am I right?"

Alec rubbed the back of his neck. "Okay, look. I don't know how long this thing with Molly will last, but I'm betting it'll be short and very sweet. This summer when I don't have class and Molly's no longer around, I can work more hours and make up what I lose now." He gazed at his friend. "I swear to you, if you were in my shoes, you'd do exactly what I'm doing."

"I doubt it. But I'll take your Thursday-night gig."

"I appreciate it, Josh." Alec smiled in gratitude. "Well, I need to head home and hit the books."

"So you can stagger to class at eight with some idea of what they're talking about, I'll bet."

"Something like that."

Josh sighed. "Here, give me the Town Car keys and I'll put them in the drop box for you. You go on home, you sorry bastard."

Alec chuckled. "Thanks." He handed over his keys and started toward his Blazer.

"And try to get her out of your system fast, will you?" Josh called after him. "You're making me very nervous, here."

"I'll do my best," Alec called back. But as he drove the silent streets to his small apartment, he thought about Molly the entire time. Considering the way she'd taken over his life, he doubted he'd be getting her out of his system all that fast. A better question was whether he'd be able to get her out of his system at all.

AS MOLLY WALKED HOME from the camera shop, she had never felt more alive. The warm weather had prodded daffodils and tulips into bloom in front yards all along her route. Although she couldn't see Long Island Sound from town, she could smell the fresh salt air blowing in off the water. Seagulls wheeled overhead, and she promised herself a trip to the beach soon.

But not today. Today she would find out if she was a wild woman or a frightened mouse. She'd tried to fool herself while renting the video equipment by telling the clerk her supposed plans for the camera and tripod. She'd concocted a story about a happy-birthday video to send to her parents, who actually did have birthdays a week apart, although they were both in August.

What a joke. You didn't send a home video to a former movie star and an Oscar-winning director. The prospect made her cringe. She did her birthday shopping for her parents at Saks.

But the clerk didn't know that, and she'd gushed about what a great present this would be. It would be a great present to herself, Molly decided, if she could actually go through with it. In the clear light of day, she doubted she could, but the idea certainly made her world more vivid.

Or maybe it was the writing she'd done this morning that was giving her this unbelievable high. She'd been inspired to write a new scene for her book, and she thought it was pretty darn hot. She could hardly wait for Alec to read it.

Or maybe it was Alec himself who made her feel as if she could leap tall buildings in a single bound. As a lover, he was ten times better than she'd imagined he'd be. She was worried about him missing his classes, though. She shouldn't have let him talk her into getting together today, but...she wanted him. Desperately.

Once he arrived, she ought to sit him down and find out exactly how much he had to do in order to get through the semester with good grades. Maybe she could help him in some way. Mostly she had to make sure that being with her wasn't jeopardizing his course work, no matter how much they both craved the contact.

Back in her little cottage, she set the box containing the equipment on the oak floor and went to prepare the bedroom. She changed sheets three times before deciding that the lace-trimmed eggshell would photograph the best. She'd been cursed with listening to movie talk all her life, and now she couldn't forget what she'd unconsciously learned. She was, after all, preparing a movie set.

With that in mind, she stripped the antique nightstands of all personal items. Then she pulled down the linen shade over the lace-curtained window and turned on the twin lamps. Not bad. If they put the tripod on the right side of the bed in front of the window, the ambient light would be nearly perfect.

Then she groaned. As if she'd really end up in that bed with Alec, being filmed in any kind of light. She couldn't do this. She really couldn't do this.

The phone rang, and she hurried to answer it. If Alec was canceling, she'd take back the video equipment this afternoon. She wasn't dealing with this well to begin with, and she definitely couldn't handle a postponement.

But Dana was on the line, not Alec.

"Hi, sweetie! How's the new book coming along?" she asked immediately.

"Uh, great, great!" Molly hadn't written a page of the new book yet. "How's life treating you, Dana?"

"Oh, sweetheart, I met a new man."

"Sounds promising." Molly didn't have high hopes, though. Dana had been meeting and rejecting men for as long as Molly had known her. Dana's first true love, an actor on the rise in the sixties, had died in a scuba accident. That was more than thirty years ago, but Dana still kept his picture on her dressing table. Molly didn't think anyone else would ever measure up.

"Jim's a sweetheart," Dana said. "But as you know, I'm picky."

Molly laughed. "You should be. You can have your choice of a boatload of guys, so why not be discriminating?"

"That's what I say. Anyway, Jim is...looking good. For the time being, anyway."

For the time being. That described her situation with Alec, too. "Nothing wrong with that." But already she wanted more than a temporary fling.

"Nope, nothing wrong with that," Dana said. "Live for the moment. At least that's what the gurus all say. Listen, I didn't call to tell you about my love life. I called because I have a dynamite idea. I think the killer should be the maid, Sophie, not the real estate guy."

"Sophie?" Molly thought of the continuing character she'd lavished so much care on book after book. Funny, irreverent Sophie could not be the killer. It would be totally against her character, and besides, she'd be out of any future books. Molly loved Sophie.

"Nobody would guess Sophie!" Dana laughed happily. "It's brilliant!"

"Um, I agree, nobody would guess Sophie, but—"

"You're hesitating. Are you so far into the book that you can't make the change?"

"Well, no, but—"

"Excellent. I can tell you'll need some convincing about this. When can you fly out so we can brainstorm over lunch and a couple of very dry martinis?"

"Well, actually, I—"

"This week isn't good for me, but next week is free."

"Dana, maybe I need to get a few more pages done before we meet." Molly imagined the marathon writing session she'd need to produce something for Dana to see.

"No, I don't want you to do another thing on this until we've had a face-to-face. Plus—oh, this is perfect—I talked to your mother yesterday and your dad is due back from Ireland this weekend. Cybil was asking if I thought you'd be coming home again anytime soon. Your dad has to fly to New Zealand in two weeks, so you'd better catch him while you can."

Molly couldn't see a way out of this. Dana would keep at her until she made the trip, and she hadn't seen her dad in months because he always seemed to be on location whenever she was home. "Okay."

"I'll book you a flight for Monday, how's that?"

"Tuesday," Molly said automatically. She always traveled on Tuesdays, Thursdays or the weekend, because those were the days Alec didn't have classes.

"Tuesday, then. And the car service I hired for you is still working out?"

Molly glanced at the box of video equipment. "So far."

"Good. I'm relieved that you're not taking chances learning to drive in unfamiliar territory. Well, think about Sophie. She's the perfect killer. Now I have to run, nail appointment in ten minutes. G'bye, sweetie."

"'Bye, Dana." Molly hung up the phone and took a deep breath. This was why she had to sell a book of her own, a book in which she had complete control over what the characters did and what they said. She'd talk Dana out of making Sophie the killer in the new book, but she might have to compromise some other plot element, and then she'd have to write around a new obstacle.

Alec seemed to think that filming themselves having sex would give her unique ideas for the scenes in her book. He could be right. If he was right, then she'd be a fool to let her inhibitions get in the way of her career as a writer.

Her mind made up, she walked over, picked up the box and carried it into the bedroom. If they were going to make this video, they might as well do a halfway decent job of it. Of the two of them, she was the one with the expertise to make sure that happened.

9

So far Alec's day hadn't been great, but it was about to get better. He was minutes away from Molly's house. Getting to this point, though, had been a little rocky.

Sometime after four in the morning, he'd fallen asleep while trying to study. He'd overslept and walked in late to class. Then he'd compounded that error by dozing off during the lecture. The professor had nudged him awake after everyone else had left. Now Alec would need to ace the final for sure if he expected to pass.

He'd also intended to ask a friend in that class if he could borrow her notes from the two afternoon sessions he'd be missing. But the lecture hall had been empty, so he'd lost that opportunity. Oh, well. He'd get the notes somehow.

In the meantime, thanks to the unplanned shut-eye, he was wide awake and ready to spend some quality time with Molly. He wondered if she'd rented the video equipment. Even if she had, he might have to spend some time convincing her to use it.

He knew exactly how he'd convince her, too. Once she was worked up, she would agree to almost anything he asked. He knew this video was a great idea, and getting her to go along would be a stimulating challenge. ·

The route to her house was familiar, but he felt really

strange parking his Blazer instead of the Town Car in front of her cottage. She'd never seen his black truck, he realized. Maybe he should have washed it.

Yeah, right. He was lucky he'd had time to wash himself, let alone his vehicle. After he'd overslept, he'd taken a very quick shower and thrown on whatever clothes were handy before dashing off. Fortunately he'd had time to go back to his apartment, take a longer shower and shave before setting out for Molly's.

Deciding what to wear had been an interesting exercise, too. She'd never seen him in anything but the Red Carpet logo shirt and dark slacks. His wardrobe wasn't fancy, but the forest-green shirt and khaki pants he had on now were his favorite outfit. He didn't expect to have it on long, but first impressions were important.

By the time he stood on her porch and rang the doorbell, he was pretty damn excited. No matter what Josh said, any guy who chose the classroom over getting naked with a woman like Molly had to be either an idiot or gay. Alec didn't regret his decision for a second.

"The door's open!" Molly called from inside the house. *Way* inside the house. From her bedroom, maybe?

Alec's heart pounded faster as he opened the door and walked into her flowered, frilly living room. He knew she'd inherited the cottage from a beloved grandmother who'd passed away, and the place looked like a grandmother had decorated it. Alec decided not to think about the grandma for the next few hours.

"I'm in here, Alec," Molly called again.

This time he was positive she was in the bedroom. Maybe she was setting up the equipment. He headed eagerly in that direction. Or maybe...

Maybe she had everything ready. He paused in the doorway and gulped. Apparently she wouldn't need any convincing.

She'd stripped the bed down to a fitted bottom sheet, and pillows cushioned the walnut headboard. The smooth ivory sheet and the lace-trimmed pillows made the perfect backdrop for Molly Drake, sex goddess.

Smiling, she lay propped against the pillows, her red hair loose and curling around her shoulders. Her bra and panties were a cool mint green. The satin material, the subtle use of underwire and the daring cut all combined to showcase the hottest body he'd ever had the privilege of ogling.

She gestured toward the window. "Camera's on," she said.

His gaze swung to the video camera mounted on a tripod to the right of the bed and in front of the shaded window. If she hadn't pointed it out, he might never have noticed. He was completely mesmerized by the sight of her lying there waiting for him, her breasts quivering with each breath.

"Come over beside the bed while you undress," she said. Her voice was breathy, but she seemed very sure of what she wanted. "I want that on film."

Somehow he hadn't expected the room to be filled with so much light. If he hadn't been so eager to join her on that bed, he might have given in to a sudden touch of stage fright. He'd pictured rolling around with her on the bed while the camera was on, but he hadn't imagined taking off his clothes in front of it.

"That shirt looks good on you," she said. "But I want it off."

Drawing a shaky breath, he thought a moment about what he was about to do. Then he nudged off his shoes and pulled off his socks before walking to the left side of the bed where he'd be within camera range. He couldn't imagine how taking off your shoes and socks could ever be sexy.

"A little to the right." She sounded like a movie director.

"If I didn't know better, I'd swear you'd done this before."

"Are you still hung up on the X-rated movie thing? Because I have not, nor will I ever be—"

"I know, Molly." Anyone who made those movies wouldn't have almost fainted at the idea of spending the afternoon in a hotel room with him. "But the way you've set everything up looks almost...professional."

Wariness flashed briefly in her eyes. "I know a...little something about movie-making."

"Were you a film student in L.A.?" He pulled his shirt from his pants and started unbuttoning, ready to have this part over with so they could get to the good stuff.

"No."

"A starlet?" Maybe she'd bombed out and come East to lick her wounds.

"No, definitely not. Slow down there, okay?"

He paused midway down the row of buttons. "Why?"

"Because it's sexier if you do. Because then..." She paused and cleared her throat. "Then I have to wait a little before I get to see you naked," she said softly. "I have time to get frustrated."

Heat rushed through him. "I've never...never tried to do a..." He didn't know the right word for when a guy stripped for a woman.

"A striptease," she said, her voice unsteady. "That's okay. I've never asked a man to do it for me, either."

"Good." He prayed to God he wouldn't look like a fool. "Then you won't know if I do it wrong."

"I don't think you could," she murmured, her gaze hot.

He had a sudden idea that would reduce the pressure on him. "Maybe you should tell me how you want me to take my clothes off."

Her gaze met his. "All right." She swallowed and looked him up and down, lingering on his crotch.

"You might want a different order than what I'd choose." He expected her to tell him to unzip his fly, from the expression of lust in her eyes.

"I think you should start with...your watch."

"My watch?" He'd totally forgotten he was wearing one.

"I want to see you unbuckle it and put it on the night-stand. Deliberately. While you're looking at me."

"My watch. Okay." He didn't get it, but as he followed her directions, he realized that it didn't matter what he took off, because every item brought them closer to incredible sex. Tension crackled between them as he laid his watch on the nightstand with a soft click. "Next?"

She directed her attention to his chest. "Unfasten another button on your shirt."

He did.

"Now the next one. Take it out of the buttonhole very slowly."

One by one, he undid the buttons at her command, his fingers trembling a little. At last the shirt hung open. As the air touched his skin, he realized he was sweating.

"Now take off your shirt, but do it gradually."

He followed her instructions while she kept her gaze

focused on his chest. She ran her tongue over her lips, and his nipples tightened. The shirt rustled to the floor behind him.

Her intense gaze warmed his skin wherever it touched. "Do you...work out?"

"No. Don't have time."

"But you're so—"

"My..." He was short of breath and had to pause. "My landlady has a fireplace, so I chop wood in exchange for a break on the rent."

"That explains all those muscles. Now unbuckle your belt."

He'd been proficient with buckles for a good many years now. He was determined to unfasten this one without watching what he was doing. After all, this would be on *tape*, for God's sake. Good thing she'd wanted him to strip slow, because unbuckling his belt took forever.

"Now pull it out of the belt loops and hand it to me."

His mouth went dry. She was thinking of more bondage games, and he was perfectly willing, but he couldn't understand how they'd manage it. "You don't have a four-poster."

"That isn't what I want it for. Give it to me and I'll show you what I have in mind."

The huskiness of her voice told him it would be wild. She was going to give him a heart attack, he decided as he pulled the belt free. Nobody's heart should be beating this fast, and he was having trouble breathing, too. He leaned over and laid the belt in her outstretched hand, wondering what she had in mind and knowing it might send him spiraling out of control.

"Thanks." A steady flame burned in her green eyes. "Soft belt. Not too wide, either. Nice." She made a loop of it and brushed it idly over the mint-green satin covering her breasts.

He shivered as he watched her drag the brown leather over her cleavage. "What...next?"

"Start unfastening your slacks." She opened her hand and the tail end of the belt unfurled, landing between her thighs.

He fumbled with the button while keeping his gaze on the belt. He was beginning to get a clue what she was planning for it. Sure enough, she slipped the end under her thigh and pulled the belt up snug between her legs. Frozen in place, he stared, his heart pounding, as she slid it slowly back and forth over that mint-green triangle covering the source of her pleasure...and his.

"You're not stripping," she murmured.

He gulped and carefully lowered his zipper, sliding it slowly past his straining penis. Damn, she was really enjoying herself with that belt. Her cheeks bloomed with color and her breathing quickened.

"Let your slacks drop to the floor."

His slacks hit the oak planks, the coins in his pocket landing with a soft jingle.

"Now your briefs."

He shoved them down, his attention riveted on the belt moving gently between her legs. "Are...are you going to...to make yourself—"

"Yes," she whispered. "And you get to watch me do it, you lucky man."

He moaned and clenched his fists at his sides. This would be a definite first for him. No woman had ever offered such a performance, and he'd never asked. But he'd wanted to ask. And now...

She tightened her hold on the belt and closed her eyes. "When you're ready...condoms...in the...drawer."

Oh, he was ready, all right, but the thrill of watching her masturbate overshadowed everything else. A hurricane could blow the roof off, for all he cared. Molly was putting on a show for him, and he was an extremely grateful audience of one.

She plucked the drenched bit of green satin aside so the leather came in direct contact with her heat. Arching slightly off the bed, she worked the leather in tight. Then she slid it back and forth while Alec stood beside the bed, his body clenched, his breathing labored.

Then, with a low moan, she lifted her hips and pulled the belt in even tighter. A few quick strokes, a sharp little cry, and she shuddered in the grip of her climax. Slowly she sank back to the mattress and gasped for air. "Now," she whispered.

The single word galvanized him into action. Wild for her, he turned and wrenched the drawer open, pulling it completely out of the nightstand. Not caring that it clattered to the floor, he leaned down and grabbed the box of condoms. Ripping the box in half, he sent packets flying while managing to snag one. In seconds he'd opened the package and rolled the latex over his erection.

Molly was still whimpering from her climax when he crawled in beside her. The belt joined the rest of his stuff on the floor. Her panties had already made way for the belt, so they were no barrier to his penis as he nudged her thighs apart, braced his hands on either side of her shoulders and slid deep.

"Oh, Alec," she said breathlessly, looking into his eyes. "I did it."

"No kidding." He pumped rhythmically, knowing

he had mere seconds before his climax. "You are so hot. You're wrecking my control."

She gripped his bottom and lifted to meet him, thrust for thrust. "That's good."

"It's beyond good." He struggled to hold back the tidal wave about to engulf him.

But she wasn't helping at all. She wrapped her legs around his and urged him on. "Come for me, Alec. I want to watch you lose it like you just watched me."

He didn't mean to satisfy that request, but when she rotated her hips with the next thrust, that did it. With a strangled cry he buried himself inside her warmth and submitted to the inevitable. Ah, what a glorious sensation as her body absorbed his wild spasms.

But when he gradually descended from that incredible high, he looked into her eyes and sighed with regret. "I wanted you to—"

"I will." She raised her head from the pillow and kissed him softly. "Many times. We have all afternoon...and hours of tape."

As THE AFTERNOON continued, Molly discovered that the more she dared, the more daring she felt. The same seemed to be true of Alec. Sometimes they forgot the camera was on, and other times they deliberately positioned themselves so that what they'd decided to try would be very clear on tape.

But Molly had removed the alarm clock from the nightstand when she'd eliminated all personal items, and it wasn't until she realized how long the shadows had become that she thought about time at all. As she was lying wrapped in Alec's arms, relaxed and well satisfied, she suddenly remembered he had a driving assignment.

She sat up, glancing wildly around for where she'd put the clock. "What time is it?"

Alec opened sleepy eyes. "I don't think we need to change the tape yet."

"Alec, your watch! Get it! You have to be somewhere tonight, and I've totally lost track of—"

"Ack!" He bounded to a sitting position and snatched his watch from the nightstand. "Omigod. I have to go."

"Will you be late?"

"Not if I haul ass." He leaped from the bed and started pulling on his clothes at breakneck speed. "Damn. I wanted to see at least part of the video before I left."

She smiled at his automatic assumption that would be happening. Clever. "I don't remember saying that you could."

"Aw, *Molly*."

He sounded so much like a disappointed little boy that she laughed. "But I guess you can, if you're good."

"You told me at least twice this afternoon that I'm very good." He grabbed his pants and stepped into them.

"Then maybe I'll let you see the video. Tell you what, I'll watch it tonight and decide if you should be allowed."

He glanced over at her in surprise. "You mean you'd actually watch it without me?"

"I thought this was supposed to be for my research?"

"It is." He tucked in his shirt and buttoned his pants. "But even though that's how it started, the thing is—"

"You're becoming a wild man and you kind of like it."

"Yeah." He grinned at her as he zipped his pants.

"Yeah, I do. And I think both of us should be seeing it for the first time, so one of us doesn't have an advantage over the other one. If we look totally goofy, we should suffer that together. That's only fair."

"Maybe, but I don't know how soon you'll be able to come over again, and I can't imagine having that tape sitting here and not taking a peek. That's asking a lot."

He paused, as if considering his options. "I'll come back tonight, after I finish my gig."

She wanted that more than anything, but she couldn't believe it was a good idea. "You need sleep and time to study. I'm sure you're already behind on both of those things."

"Listen, I can study while I wait for these folks to finish their dinner, so there's some time made up right there. And I don't have class tomorrow, and no driving assignments tomorrow night. I'll come over tonight, we'll watch the tape, and then I'll go home, catch some z's and study some more. How's that?"

"You're burning the candle at both ends, Alec."

He smiled. "It's your fault for being so hot, Molly."

"See there? You just admitted that I'm interfering with your—"

"No, you're not. I'm teasing. This will work. Will you leave the tape alone until I can get here?"

"When will that be?"

"No later than midnight."

Having him show up at midnight had an illicit feel that she loved. "I guess I could get some writing done between now and then." She had a feeling her fingers would fly over the keys. "I meant to show you what I wrote this morning."

"Give it to me now. I can read it tonight."

She shook her head. "You're supposed to be studying, not reading my manuscript."

"I doubt you wrote *that* much. Come on, let me see it. Ten minutes of reading your book isn't going to make that much difference."

She had to agree that her six pages of material shouldn't take long to read. "Okay, I'll get them." She climbed from the bed. Her cottage was secluded, with greenery sheltering her windows from the road and her neighbors' windows, so she could walk naked into the living room. She'd never done it before, but today it seemed like the natural thing.

As she passed Alec on her way into the hall, she swayed her hips and hoped he'd noticed. His sharp intake of breath was gratifying. She liked knowing he was following her down the hall. She was turning into such a wanton wench.

"The pages are right here." She picked up the pages where she'd left them lying on the coffee table.

Behind her, Alec groaned, and she turned around as if she had no idea what could be the matter. Glancing at the bulge behind his fly, she smiled.

"You did all that on purpose."

"Did what?" She batted her eyes at him.

"You sex kitten, you." He ran a hand over his face. "Keeping my distance when you walked past me was tough enough, but then I had to follow you in here and watch you lean over."

Her body tightened with desire. "You'd think we'd have had enough of each other," she said, her voice low and husky.

"You would think so, wouldn't you?" His gaze swept over her. "But if I thought I could find somebody to take this assignment, I would. And then I'd explore the possibilities of having you lean over like that again."

Her breath caught. She could easily imagine the scene, and the eroticism of it made her slippery with desire...again.

"You'd like that, wouldn't you, Molly?" he asked softly.

"You'll be late." She handed him the pages.

"Standing here looking at you, I can't get myself to care."

She could feel herself sliding toward the same reckless abandon. She forced herself to think of his job. "Then I'll leave the room, so you can get out of here. Go on, Alec. I'll see you soon."

"Not nearly soon enough," he murmured as she walked into the bedroom and quietly shut the door.

A moment later she heard him leave. She gazed at the rumpled bed, empty now, and the camera they'd never shut off. No matter how she tried to escape it, she was a Hollywood kid. All those years of being around her parents made her want to tie up this video in some dramatic way.

Alec's belt was still on the floor. She walked over, picked it up and tossed it on the bed, as a kind of symbolic statement. But that lacked punch. Laughing to herself, she climbed up on the mattress. "The end," she said, and mooned the camera. Just for Alec.

She was still grinning when she turned the machine off and went to take a long, hot shower. Her wild woman was alive and well and turning Alec inside out. She was having the time of her life, and she most definitely did not want to go to L.A. next week.

10

MOLLY TRIED TO FORGET that Alec had her six-page love scene with him and could be reading it at any moment. Whenever she remembered, her stomach churned nervously. Writing another love scene for her book helped distract her, but whenever she took a break, her case of nerves came galloping back.

She thought those six pages were better than what she'd done before, but if Alec didn't think so, that would be devastating. A little after eleven the phone rang and she hurried to answer it.

"This is a heavy breather," Alec said. "I'd like to make an obscene phone call. Are you interested?"

She knew she was supposed to laugh, but all she cared about was his reaction to her work. "Um, have you read those pages I gave you?"

"That's why you're getting the obscene phone call, little lady. What you wrote got me so excited I thought about taking care of myself right here in the limo."

"*Really?* Woo-hoo!" She laughed and did a quick dance step around the telephone stand. "That's wonderful!"

"Easy for you to say. You're not sitting in the driver's seat of an expensive stretch limo with your privates in a state of high anxiety."

"Oh, Alec, I'm so sorry."

"You don't sound sorry."

"I am. I truly am. But I love your reaction to my scene. Were you serious about...taking care of yourself right there?" She quivered at the thought.

"No, unfortunately. My customers could come out of the nightclub any minute. I have to start reading my family law textbook if I hope to be in any condition to get out and open the door for them."

Molly ran her tongue over her lips. "I want you. I want you bad."

He groaned. "Don't say things like that on the phone, Molly."

"I never have before."

"Now's not the time to start."

"Yeah, but I wanted to try it out and see how it felt to talk sexy on the phone." She wiggled with pleasure as her inner wild woman gave her a high five. "It was fun."

"Fun for you, maybe. Frustrating as hell for me."

"Hey, wasn't this supposed to be an obscene phone call? So far you haven't said one obscene thing to me, Alec."

"I want to lick you all over."

She could almost feel the hot lap of his tongue. "Good, that's a start."

"But I can't until I drive these party animals home. We've been to three clubs so far and I'm afraid they may have at least one more in mind."

"That's too bad."

"I know. Don't get me wrong. They're a great bunch, and normally I'm really into the idea of chauffeuring happy people out to have a good time. Just not tonight. Tonight I want to be with you."

The statement struck a chord in her, making her warm in ways that had nothing to do with sex. She realized that she wanted to be with him, too, and not only because of what they'd do in bed. She simply enjoyed his company. "They'll have to go home sometime."

"They will. They all have to work tomorrow, but even so, it might be past midnight. Can I still come over?"

This conversation was becoming very cozy, as if they were a couple. For Alec's sake, she decided it was time to swing it back to their original purpose in seeing each other. "You can still come...over. And over. And—"

"Cut it out, Molly. This isn't funny. You should see the way my pants stick out."

She smiled. "What you need is a good lap dance."

"What I need is to hang up this cell phone. But here I am, torturing myself because I love hearing your voice."

"You do?" It was the sort of comment a real boy-friend would make. Despite the obstacles, she was be-ginning to think of him that way, too. Maybe, if she was careful not to interfere with his studies, they had a chance.

"Yeah, I do." He sounded a little startled by the fact, himself. "It's a good voice. Musical, almost. Do you sing?"

"Only in the shower."

"I remember some other things you like to do in the shower."

"*Now* who's causing trouble?" She wondered if he'd returned to the topic of sex on purpose, to avoid getting too emotionally intimate.

"You're the bad influence, you and these six pages you talked me into reading."

"I did not! You insisted on—"

"Hey." He chuckled. "I know. I was teasing you."

"Oh." The sound of his soft chuckle touched a well-guarded place in her heart, a place she'd originally meant to keep strictly separate from this sexual adventure of theirs. A true wild woman would have been able to do that and indulge in a brief affair, no strings attached. Apparently she wasn't wild through and through, because she couldn't imagine dropping Alec once she had the experience she needed to write a better book.

"Molly? You still there?"

"Uh-huh."

"I wondered. You got quiet all of a sudden. Listen, are you getting sleepy? Maybe I shouldn't come by, if you're too tired. I don't want—"

"I'm not sleepy." And his consideration only added to the feeling of emotional intimacy. He had to sense what was happening, too, yet he wasn't backing away. She probably shouldn't hope for their relationship to become something more, but she couldn't help it. "And I wouldn't be able to sleep without watching that tape, anyway."

"Me, neither. Whoops, here come my charges. I'll get there when I can, okay?"

"I'll be waiting."

"I'm counting on that. 'Bye, Molly." He hung up before she could say anything else.

She pictured him tucking away his cell phone and leaping out of the limo. Other people besides her probably requested Alec as their driver, not because they were hot for him, but because he was so cheerful and accommodating. He certainly had the right personality for what he'd chosen as a part-time job to get him through law school. Come to think of it, he was more enthusiastic about his job than he'd ever been about school, but that was understandable. His class work had to be tough.

Damn, but he was such a nice guy. Life would be far simpler if he happened to be a jerk who looked wonderful and was fabulous in bed. Instead, he was perfect for her. She might even be perfect for him, except that right now she had to be putting a strain on his schedule.

She couldn't stop worrying about the bad influence she might be on him, especially near the end of the semester like this. At least on Tuesday she'd be heading to California for several days. Breaking off with him before she left might be the smartest move for both of them, but apparently she wasn't that smart. The prospect of a mere five days left in their adventure made her realize that she didn't want it to end.

ALEC WAS OPERATING on pure adrenaline by the time he parked his Blazer in front of Molly's house at one in the morning. He still wore his chauffeur's uniform, although he'd left the hat on the seat of the Blazer. She'd never seen him in this getup because he'd never driven her anywhere in the stretch limo. As he walked up to her door with her manuscript pages in one hand, he loosened the knot of his tie with the other hand, pulling it down a few inches so he could unfasten the top button of his dress shirt.

She opened the door wearing a white satin bathrobe and her feet were bare. The sash tied snugly around her waist pulled the smooth material taut over her breasts. Instantly all tiredness left him.

"Hi," she said softly, and stepped back so he could enter.

The feeling of homecoming was so strong that he couldn't speak, couldn't even return her simple greet-

ing. Still clutching the manuscript pages in one hand, he
swept her into his arms the minute she'd closed the
door. God, how he'd missed her.

He covered her face with kisses and breathed in the
flower and citrus scent of soap and shampoo. If Molly
could be waiting at the door for him every night...no, he
had no business thinking that way.

But he couldn't get enough of her. He nuzzled behind
her ear and the curve of her throat. "You smell delicious."

She molded her body to his as she worked him out of
his fitted jacket. "I took a shower and washed my hair
to wake myself up."

He should feel guilty that she'd had to work to keep
herself awake for him, but he was too busy using his
free hand to untie her sash and touch her under the slippery material of her robe. When he cupped her bare
breast, he groaned. "Molly, I need—"

"Me, too." She reached for his zipper. "Just to take
the edge off."

"After that we'll watch the tape." He slipped his
hand between her thighs and discovered he wasn't the
only one with constant cravings.

"Mmm, good." Her voice was a low croon as she
moved her hips lazily, encouraging his exploration.

"You're so wet."

"And how about you?" she murmured. "Are you as
ready as I am?"

"More."

"Glad to hear it." Gazing into his eyes, she reached in
through his open fly. He gasped as she found the opening of his briefs and curled her fingers around his erection. "I do love a man in uniform." Then she carefully
eased his penis free.

He closed his eyes in ecstasy as she stroked him with hands that had learned how he liked it. "We...we should get a..."

"Right here."

He opened his eyes just as she released him and backed away a step so she could take a condom from the pocket of her robe. Knowing that she'd stashed it there in anticipation of this moment gave his ego such a boost he might never be humble again.

"You can drop those pages you're holding," she said as she ripped open the packet and moved in close so she could roll the condom on. "I think you're going to need two hands for this next part."

"The sofa?" He hoped so. He'd never make it to the bedroom.

"No."

"The floor?" He was a desperate man.

"The coffee table."

The pages fell from his nerveless fingers and scattered over the braided rug. Through a red haze he watched her walk to the low walnut table in front of the sofa.

She glanced over her shoulder, her eyebrows lifted. "Coming?"

"Any second." He closed the distance between them just as she leaned over and braced her hands on the table and her knees on the edge. He nearly passed out from the excitement.

She wiggled her satin-covered bottom. "Then you'd better work fast."

Breathing in ragged gasps, he pushed the slick material up and over in one quick motion. Revealing her bare bottom wrenched a moan of desire from his throat.

Need burned like a hot coal in his gut as he palmed her smooth cheeks, probed her moistness and drove home.

She'd given him an erotic fantasy he'd never expected to have come true—a lush, willing woman naked under her satin robe offering herself in the most primitive way to a man so crazed with lust he'd removed none of his clothing before taking her. The moment was carnal and wild, a time for rapid thrusting and eager cries blended with the rhythmic slap of thigh against rump.

He felt her climax draw near. Remembering that moment in the car, he gave her a pinch on her smooth bottom that sent her right over. As she trembled and cried out, he rode quickly to his own shattering orgasm. Somehow he had the presence of mind to guide them both to the braided rug soon after, where they sprawled in complete abandon. As his racing heart gradually slowed, Alec reached for Molly's hand. Silently he laced his fingers through hers and squeezed gently. She squeezed back.

That was the first time he knew. He wanted to hold on...forever.

WHEN THEY BOTH nearly fell asleep on the braided rug, Molly suggested they take a nap in her bed before watching the video. She was exhausted, and she could imagine how tired Alec must be. It was funny, she thought as they slipped naked into bed, cuddled close and pulled the covers over them. They were too busy having sex to watch a movie of themselves having sex.

She also wondered if she really needed the video. What she'd shared with Alec was stamped so deeply into her memory that she'd never forget. No video necessary.

Uninhibited sex with him had set her free to write vivid, intense scenes that excited her and apparently had the same effect on him. In a sense, the purpose of their original session in the hotel had been accomplished. But she didn't want him to know that. Maybe she wouldn't have him read any more of her manuscript just yet, she decided as she drifted off to sleep in his arms.

She awoke to sunlight outlining the edge of her bedroom window shade and the phone ringing. Jumping out of bed, she grabbed her white robe and shoved her arms into the sleeves as she hurried to answer it. With luck it wouldn't be Dana. Molly didn't want to have to lie to Alec about Dana, but she didn't feel comfortable telling him the truth, either. Dana would have to give her the okay before she'd do something like that, and Dana didn't even know Alec.

Instead, it was Alec's friend Josh, the one who'd been convinced she was an X-rated video star. Molly thought about the tape sitting beside her television set and wondered if Josh's speculation had become a self-fulfilling prophecy.

"I'm sorry to bother you," he said. "But I need to get in touch with Alec and he isn't at home. I know he often drives for you on Tuesdays and Thursdays, so although you weren't on the Red Carpet schedule for today, I thought you might be able to help me find him."

He knows. She was as sure of that as her own name. "Um, he's not scheduled to drive me anywhere today," she said, idiotically repeating what Josh already knew as she thought frantically of what she should say.

"I didn't think so. And he's not scheduled for anything else until tonight, so normally in that case he spends the day studying. But I checked his usual spot in the law library, and he's not there, either."

Molly winced at Josh's tone. Obviously he didn't approve of Alec slacking off on his studying to be with her. She didn't really approve of it, either. Blinded by lust, she'd allowed it to happen, and maybe it was a good thing Josh had called.

"I will be happy to give Alec a message if I should hear from him," she said.

"Would you do that? He asked me if I could take his driving assignment tonight, but I have a conflict, and I won't be able to do it after all. If you hear from him, could you give him that message?"

"I certainly will." Now she knew something else. Alec, who always needed extra money, was ducking out of a driving assignment, no doubt so that he could spend time with her. She needed to set some ground rules, and fast.

"Thanks, Ms. Drake. I appreciate it."

"Call me Molly." *Any friend of Alec's is a friend of mine. I hope.*

"Okay. Thanks, Molly. He should probably take this assignment if he possibly can. This particular customer is known for being a great tipper, and I'm sure he could use the money."

"Of course. Thanks again."

After Josh said a polite but reserved goodbye, Molly hung up the phone and tiptoed over to the bedroom door. Alec was still out cold, which didn't surprise her. He looked so good lying there, his brawny chest draped with a lace-trimmed top sheet, his morning beard making him seem dark and dangerous.

But she was the dangerous one. He'd been sailing along, managing to fit his studies in around his job, making progress toward his goal of becoming a lawyer. Then she'd asked him up to that hotel room and completely disrupted his schedule.

She hadn't asked him to cut class or give up a lucrative driving assignment for her, but who could blame him? He'd had his nose to the grindstone for a long time, and he'd been ripe for seduction. However, she had no intention of playing Delilah to his Samson.

Backing away from the bedroom, she decided to let him sleep. They'd talk about getting him back on track once he woke up.

"Hey," he called softly as she started down the hallway. "Where are you going?"

Emotion flooded her at the tender sound of that greeting. She wasn't used to waking up with a man in her bed, and having this particular one there thrilled her way too much.

She turned and walked back to stand in the doorway. He shoved a pillow behind his head and smiled at her. "C'mere."

"No can do." She fought the urge to climb back in bed with him. "Josh called."

His eyes snapped wide open. "Here?"

"He checked your apartment and the law library first. Then he called to see if I might know where you were."

Alec blew out a breath. "We can trust Josh. He's one of my oldest friends, and so naturally I hinted to him what was happening. I hope you don't mind."

"Of course not. I'm not the one with anything to risk. And if Josh is your friend, he won't turn you in. He did ask me to tell you he can't take your driving assignment tonight, though."

Alec looked exactly like a little boy caught with his hand in the cookie jar. "Oh."

"What were you thinking, giving away a good moneymaker to be with me? And don't pretend that's not the reason."

He gazed at her. "It's the reason. But it's no big deal to skip a gig here and there. I can make up the money this summer, when I'm not in school."

"Sorry, but I won't let you sacrifice like that just so that we—"

"Can have incredible sex?" he finished, his voice husky.

Oh, God, no woman should be asked to stand there and resist a man like Alec lying naked and willing in her bed.

"I may have to drive tonight, but that's hours away," he continued softly. "Come back to bed, Molly. It's what we both want and you know it."

"That's not the point!" She shoved her fists into the pockets of her robe. "You need to spend time studying to make up for all the hours you've already lost."

"Don't worry about that. I can—"

"I *am* worried about that. If I've messed with your schedule so much that your grades are in jeopardy, I'll never forgive myself."

He frowned and shook his head impatiently. "You haven't, Molly. If there's one thing I've learned in all these years of college, it's how to study. I'm very efficient."

"I believe that. So go home and be efficient today. I'd feel a hundred percent better if you would do that. The guilt is killing me."

He didn't budge, and from the stubborn set of his jaw, he didn't look as if he planned to. "So what about that tape? I thought we were going to watch it together."

"I promise not to watch it until we see each other again." She would put the brakes on this runaway train, somehow. The tape could wait.

His jaw remained hard, his gaze uncompromising. "And when will that be?"

"Friday night?"

"I have to work. And I suppose you'd disapprove if I tried to get a replacement."

"Do you have any jobs lined up for Saturday?" Her departure on Tuesday loomed on the horizon, but she didn't want to tell him about that yet. He might push for more time with her, and then he'd be even further behind.

"I'm taking one of the professors to the airport Saturday morning. I think that's it."

She took a deep breath. "Then I'll hire you for Saturday afternoon and Saturday night."

His eyes darkened with anger. "Damn it, Molly, you will not. If you won't see me again until Saturday, I'll try to live with that. I'll make use of the time to get all caught up on my schoolwork and get in some driving gigs, if that's what it takes to make you happy. But you are not paying me to be with you on Saturday."

She lifted her chin. "Why not? What if I have errands to run? What if I wanted to go into Mystic and browse through the shops? Do you want me to hire somebody else to take me?"

"Okay, let's say you have all these errands, which I doubt. Then I'll take you in the Blazer." He paused and pierced her with his dark gaze. "Unless my Blazer's not classy enough for you?"

He had her. Someday he would make a very good

lawyer, one who would circle around and catch a witness just like this. If she insisted on hiring him to drive the Town Car, she'd look like a snob, even though all she wanted was to help him make a living.

"All right," she said at last. "That would be great."

His expression relaxed. "Good. And now that we have that settled, come on over here. If I have to leave you alone until Saturday, I want to give you a little something to remember me by."

"I'm afraid to come over there. Once we get started, we can't seem to—"

"You think I have no self-control when it comes to you, right?"

"Well, judging from the evidence so far, that's what I think, yes. And I'm not much better regarding you. It's not a judgment, just an observation."

"I'm going to prove you wrong, Molly Drake. Take off that robe and come here. I'll make both of us feel really good, and then I'm outta here. And that's a promise."

A girl had only so much willpower. Heart thudding, Molly approached the bed, untying her sash as she walked toward him. "I'm going to trust you on this one."

"Miss Molly, you can trust me every time. And I'm about to start proving that to you."

11

LEAVING MOLLY SHORTLY after giving her a screaming orgasm was not easy, but Alec did it. His honor was at stake.

He managed to preserve the glow of his own excellent climax until he was nearly home. But when he was a few blocks from his apartment, the reality of spending the next two days without Molly sank in, and he pounded the steering wheel in frustration.

No doubt about it, he was falling for her, falling for a woman who had some mysterious life in L.A. she wouldn't talk about and a childhood she didn't care to discuss. She needed him to help her write better sex, but she was already starting to do that, judging from the six pages he'd read the night before. Soon he'd be obsolete.

He'd like to believe that she wanted the relationship to continue even after she had the experience she needed for her sex scenes. But no matter how he tried to convince himself of that, he couldn't avoid one important fact. A woman interested in building a relationship wouldn't keep whole parts of her life secret from the guy she was involved with.

He had Molly for a little while, and then she'd move on. A sense of urgency dogged him, making him worry that staying away for two days would cause their fragile connection to snap.

The minute he got inside his utilitarian little apartment he pulled out his cell phone and called her. "I just wanted you to know I'm home and about to start studying," he said. And the prospect was very unappetizing. He'd rented the efficiency apartment furnished, and from the tweed sofa bed to the scarred kitchen table, there was nothing creative or decorative about it.

"Good. You need to study." Her voice was rich and mellow, like a woman well satisfied. "You really did leave promptly, too. I barely had a chance to thank you."

He started getting hard just from listening to that musical voice of hers. He paced the tiny apartment, the cell phone to his ear. "So you liked that?"

"I think you could tell. Luckily the neighbors are some distance away, or they'd have been able to tell, too."

"Hearing you yell like that does wonders for my ego." Knowing they'd be without each other for two days, he'd prolonged their session this morning, teasing her and then backing off, building the tension to an unbearable point for both of them.

When she'd finally come, he'd nearly had to peel her off the ceiling. His release had been pretty damn spectacular, too. He'd had the satisfaction of knowing she hadn't wanted him to leave when he'd finally crawled out of her bed.

"Don't forget to eat," she said. "You should have let me fix you something."

"I'll eat. And if I'd stayed for breakfast, we would have ended up plastered against your kitchen table. After making you a promise, I didn't dare test myself that far."

"I'm impressed with your resolve."

"Thanks." He pictured her pacing around the telephone table as she talked to him. He wanted to be with her so much he ached. "What are you going to do for the next two days?" He wasn't sure he had a right to ask, but he wanted to know.

"I'll write."

"Think you can do that without watching the video?"

"Yeah," she said softly. "All I have to do is close my eyes and everything comes back to me."

"Same here." He didn't even have to close his eyes. He could still feel her touch and taste her skin.

"The video may be overkill."

"But let's watch it anyway, Saturday night."

She laughed. "Saturday night at the movies."

"Yeah. I'll bring popcorn."

"Maybe you should just bring the oil."

"Now, there's an idea." He was so into that image that he jumped when his doorbell buzzed. "Molly, somebody's at the door. Hold on and I'll—"

"No, I'll hang up now. We could talk forever, and you need to work."

"But—"

"'Bye, Alec." The line went dead.

With a soft curse he disconnected his cell and walked to the door. But he thought it was interesting that she'd said they could talk forever. It almost sounded as if she liked him for reasons other than sex.

Josh stood on the other side of the door. "Good. You're home."

"And it's all your fault. Because of your phone call, she kicked me out."

Josh walked into the apartment, not waiting for an invitation. "I figured you were there when I couldn't find you."

Alec closed the door with a sigh. "You leaned on her,

didn't you? Made her feel guilty for taking me away from work and school."

"I just mentioned the obvious, that you were giving up a lot of money by trying to palm off your driving assignment on somebody else. I didn't say a word about the school thing."

"Damn it, Josh. Couldn't you have simply left a message for me to call you? I know you think you're trying to help, but I..." *I could still be rolling around in bed with Molly right now.* "I can handle this myself."

"Think so?" Josh's gray eyes swept over him. "You were in such a rush to get over to her house you didn't even ditch the monkey suit first. I've never known you to wear that outfit ten seconds longer than necessary. I think you're in over your head, buddy."

"Maybe that's how I like it."

"Well, try this on for size." Josh flopped down on the sofa, hooked an ankle over his knee and leaned back. "When I was in the law library I asked a couple of people if they'd seen you. One woman in your Wednesday-afternoon lecture said you missed a major test that's supposed to count for a fourth of your semester grade. Did you happen to forget about that?"

Alec groaned. "Yeah, I did." He pulled out a kitchen chair, straddling it to face Josh. "For some reason I thought it was next Wednesday."

"I think I know what that reason was. She has red hair and a beautiful pair of—"

"Watch yourself."

"Eyes. I was gonna say eyes."

Alec glared at him. "I certainly hope so."

"Whew. This is way worse than I thought. I haven't seen you this territorial in a long time. Didn't you say this relationship would be short and sweet?"

"I really don't want to talk about it, Josh."

Josh leaned his head back and stared at the ceiling. "Okay. Your funeral." He lifted his head and pushed himself up. "Guess I'll take off and leave you to mop up after yourself. I think you might want to see if your professor for that lecture class has office hours today."

"For a guy who has no interest in college, you sure are an expert on the process." Alec got up from the chair.

"Hey, I learned all the tricks during my one glorious semester, remember? I happen to hate going to school, but if I thought it would matter whether I had a degree or not, I'd suffer through." He paused by Alec's front door. "There is one thing I wanted to ask you."

"If it's about Molly, I think we should drop the subject."

"It's not about Molly." Some of the swagger disappeared from Josh's stance. "It's about Pris."

Alec blinked. "Pris?" Josh hadn't talked about his old girlfriend for months, ever since he'd mentioned that she was getting married. He'd tossed the information out as if it didn't faze him, but Alec hadn't believed that for a minute. "What about her?"

"I don't know why she's doing this, but she's hired Red Carpet for the limo service to and from the church."

Alec thought it was strange, too, but he tried to pass it off as nothing. "Maybe she trusts the company to give good service," he said with a shrug.

"Yeah, but why the hell did she have to request me as a driver? That's being a real super-bitch, if you ask me."

If Alec hadn't known Josh for years, he might have missed the hurt hiding behind the anger. "Either she's out for revenge or she has a twisted sense of humor."

"Whichever it is, I don't want any part of it. I'd appreciate it if you'd step in that day. We don't have to go through Edgars, because then Pris might get wind of it and pitch a fit. But if you show up on the wedding day instead of me, she can't do a thing about it at that point."

"When is it?"

"A week from Saturday."

Alec wondered where he'd stand with Molly a week from Saturday. Maybe nowhere. They might be over. "Sure, I'll do that."

"I really appreciate it, buddy. And I'm sorry I can't take the gig for you tonight. My sister called and my nephew's getting an award at school tonight. She wants the whole family there, so I'm driving up to Hartford this afternoon. Ryan's a good kid, and I—"

"No problem." Now that Alec knew about the test he'd spaced, he realized he had to spend some time getting his life in order. He still didn't like being away from Molly, but if he didn't straighten out a few details he really might put the semester in jeopardy. "Thanks for finding out about the test and say hi to Suzanne and the rest of the family for me."

"Will do." With a sloppy salute, Josh opened the door and left.

Alec gazed at the closed door for several seconds after Josh left. Unless he didn't know Josh at all, his friend still had feelings for Pris. But when she'd pressured him for a ring last year, he'd bailed and she'd been heartbroken. Maybe she was doing this to prove she was totally over Josh. Whatever her reason, Alec didn't want to give her the opportunity to zing his friend.

With a sigh he headed for the shower, stripping off his starched dress shirt on the way. He'd never cared

much for the monkey suit, but now he'd always associ-
ate it with Molly. Once he'd stepped into the shower,
there was the bar of hotel soap to bring him more memories of her. She'd worked her way into his life and under his skin. Next stop—his heart.

MOLLY WAS BLINDSIDED by how much she missed Alec.
The moment he left the cottage, she felt cut off from a
significant part of herself. She coped in the way she always had whenever loneliness struck—she wrote.

Fortunately for her, she had plenty to do. Besides revising the sex scenes in her novel, she had to find a different killer for the mystery she was supposed to be
writing for Dana. No way would she let Dana finger Sophie, but maybe the real estate guy wasn't a good sus-
pect, either. There was a suspicious gardener who
might suit her purposes.

After haggling over points like these with Dana
through several books, Molly had learned that if she
ditched both her original idea along with Dana's lame
contribution, she could usually sell Dana on a third al-
ternative. Part of the drill was making Dana think she'd
thought of the compromise. God love her, Dana had the
ego most stars needed to survive in Hollywood. Molly
had to play to that ego.

Working on the mystery turned out to be easier than
revising sex scenes. After a couple of hours of hot loving between the pages of her book, Molly craved even
hotter loving between the sheets of her bed. Her body's
thermostat, previously set on medium, had been turned
up to high. She'd gotten exactly what she'd asked for,
and now she was writing hot. She was also writing frustrated.

When the pressure became too much, she'd put her

own book aside and wrestle with the plot of the mystery until she'd cooled off a little. By Friday night she recognized that she might have a problem. With a goal of writing sexy novels under her own name instead of cozy mysteries under Dana's name, she was setting herself up to be permanently aroused.

Alec could handle that problem beautifully for her, but she couldn't count on Alec to lower her frustration level on a regular basis. He was a very busy guy, and would continue to be busy for some time to come. But she didn't want anybody else for the job.

She'd never considered that getting the experience to write the way she wanted would trip a switch inside that now seemed welded permanently in the *on* position. Or that the one man who could put out the fire would have too many other pressing things to do.

In any case, she couldn't go back, couldn't erase that afternoon in the hotel room, nor would she want to. Life was more intense now, and she liked that. Instinctively she knew this affair would make her a better writer, even if it made her crazy and broke her heart.

WHEN SATURDAY FINALLY arrived, she waited eagerly, counting the minutes until Alec would appear. When they'd talked on Thursday, she'd pretended to have errands today, when in fact she had none. But she was embarrassed to admit to him that she was willing to spend their entire time together in bed, so she'd dressed for an outing and was determined they'd have one.

Her short, flouncy skirt had flowers on it in honor of spring, and her green blouse was the color of new leaves. She'd even added a wide-brimmed straw hat that definitely announced they were going out, not staying in. Maybe she wouldn't look as desperate for his touch as she felt.

At one-thirty his black Blazer rumbled to a stop in front of her house. Heart racing, she grabbed her summer straw purse and went out the door. They met in the middle of the flagstone walkway.

He reached for her, gripping her by both arms, his eyes hidden by his aviator shades, his expression tense. "God, Molly." His fingers flexed. "You wouldn't believe how much I've missed you."

She swallowed. "I probably would." She trembled, wondering if they should just go back in and quit pretending they were civilized human beings.

His gaze flicked to her hat. "I guess you weren't kidding about the errands."

Yes, I was. Take me now. "No. I need to go to Mystic and look for some gifts for my parents." Gifts for her parents had become her all-purpose excuse, apparently.

A muscle twitched in his jaw. "All right, then. Let's go." He kept a grip on her elbow as they walked toward his truck.

The underside was rusty from too many New England winters spent on salt-packed roads, but the part that still retained a finish gleamed from a recent wash and wax job. Her conscience pricked her. Alec didn't have time to clean his vehicle.

But he'd done it, and she should at least let him know she'd noticed. "Your truck looks good." She took off her hat so she wouldn't knock it off when she got in.

"As good as it can, considering it's about ready to be put out to pasture." He opened the door and helped her into the Blazer with the same flourish he used with the elegant Town Car, reminding her to buckle up before he closed the door.

She set her purse on the floor and her hat in her lap. She'd bet the interior had been vacuumed recently, too. The worn upholstery didn't have a speck of dirt on it. He'd gone to all that trouble for her, she was sure, just in case he ended up taking her somewhere today. She was very glad she'd followed up on the errand plan so his effort hadn't gone to waste.

Alec climbed behind the wheel and closed his door. "Maybe I shouldn't do this, but I have to." He leaned over and kissed her.

Immediately lost to the world, she whimpered and clutched his head to bring him closer.

With a groan he thrust his tongue deep. Then, before the kiss could turn into something else, he pulled away, cleared his throat and started the engine. Soft jazz, their usual traveling music, came from the tape player. He might not have a CD changer, but he'd made sure they had their music, all the same.

As he drove away from her cottage, he glanced at her. "Notice that I had the discipline to stop kissing you, even though I wanted to rip your clothes off."

Still reeling from the kiss, she struggled for breath. "I...noticed."

"You seem determined about the errands."

"I do?"

"You wore a hat. That's a pretty clear signal that you don't want to start with the usual hanky-panky."

"Well, we have the whole day and night, so I—"

"We have all the way until tomorrow afternoon, Molly." He took a deep breath, as if hit by a case of nerves. "Unless you have an objection to putting up with me that long."

She felt like moaning with pleasure at the thought, but she didn't want to appear pathetically eager.

"Sounds good to me," she said in the understatement of the year, "but are you sure that you can spare the time?"

"I've worked my tail off since Thursday so that I could spare the time. The one thing keeping me going was the possibility I could be with you for twenty-four hours. If it's okay with you, you're my reward for good behavior."

"I'd like that." The prospect was more than fine with her, even though she knew they were both getting in deeper by spending so much time in each other's company. But maybe there was a way they could make this relationship work.

He reached over, took her hand and threaded his fingers through hers. "Me, too, Molly. I'd like that...a lot."

She loved the way her hand felt in his. They hadn't done much hand-holding, and yet it seemed like the most natural thing in the world for them to be doing it now.

"Thank you for giving me a ride in your truck today," she said.

"It's not quite what you're used to, I guess."

"The truth is, I feel honored to be riding in your truck."

He laughed. "Honored? I don't understand that at all."

"Usually you're driving me somewhere because it's your job, and the Town Car is nice, but it's... impersonal. This truck is yours, so it has more of your personality."

"I hope you're not saying I'm rusty."

"No!" She laughed. "I only—"

"Because I'll admit before Tuesday I was a little out of practice, but I think by now the machinery is oiled up pretty good." He waggled his eyebrows at her. "Don't you think?"

"I do." She grinned at him. "I wasn't talking about the rust. I was talking about the rugged, manly image of a black truck."

"Aha." He puffed out his chest. "Now we're talkin'."

"With those *big, muscular* tires."

"Yeah, baby."

"And fantastic traction on slick, slippery surfaces."

"Mmm-hmm. I love it when you talk dirty."

They had fun together, she realized. They always had. "I love watching you drive this macho truck. I have to say it suits you much better than the Town Car."

He grinned. "Thanks, I think. Here I am trying to better myself and become a fancy lawyer who buys luxury cars as a hobby, and you're saying I look more at home behind the wheel of a rusty old Blazer. Maybe I don't have the makings of a high roller."

"Being a high roller is highly overrated."

He gave her a quick glance. "And you know, don't you, Molly?"

"I do know." Riding along with her hand in his, she knew that she should tell him this much, at least. "My dad's a film director. Owen Drake."

"Holy shit." His fingers tightened in hers. "No wonder you could run a video camera."

"I've never been trained, but you can't help but pick things up."

"I'm sure. Owen Drake. Wow."

She decided that she might as well add her mother's name into the mix. "You might not know my mother, but she's—"

"Cybil O'Connor. *The Haunted Lagoon*." He looked over at her. "I can see the resemblance now."

Molly sighed. "I guess *The Haunted Lagoon* is still on every teenage boy's must-see list, huh?"

"I'll never watch it again, I swear."

"It's okay. I'm fairly used to having a mother who made one of the all-time favorite nude scenes in Hollywood history." She had a sudden thought. "But don't tell Josh any of this, okay? I try to keep a low profile. I really don't want anybody in the area to know. I'm trying to stay anonymous here."

He nodded. "I totally understand. This is safe with me."

"I knew it would be."

He was silent for a while, as if processing what she'd said. "It's funny, but one of my pipe dreams was becoming an entertainment lawyer. I thought it would be cool to go out there and mingle with the stars."

Well, there went any thoughts she might have had about telling him about the ghostwriting. People sometimes made pipe dreams come true. And just because she didn't like that life, he might, and she didn't want to give him a secret he might accidentally spill during a cocktail party in Beverly Hills.

"That probably sounds dumb to you," he said.

"Not at all. You might love it. I grew up in that world, and now I want to try and stay as far away from it as I can get."

"I can understand that, I guess. You're a private kind of person. But with your writing ability, you'd sure have the connections to get a screenplay sold." He paused. "Or is that why you go back all the time? You're writing screenplays already?"

"No, I'm not writing screenplays. I've always known

I wanted to write novels." Maybe she'd made a mistake, telling him about her dad. She should have realized that one revelation might make him want to know more about her. She held her breath, waiting for him to ask why she made so many trips back to L.A., especially considering that she didn't like the place.

Instead, he lifted her hand to his lips and kissed her fingers gently. "Thanks for telling me about your folks, Miss Molly."

He wasn't going to ask her. Her eyes misted. He was tuned in enough to know that she wouldn't tell him, even if he asked. He was respecting her boundaries. That alone would be enough to make her fall in love with him.

12

ALEC SEESAWED between delight and despair. He loved that Molly had confided in him, but he couldn't see how he'd ever bridge the gap between a guy who'd grown up in a lower-middle-class neighborhood in Hartford and a woman from one of the royal families of Hollywood. At least he'd had sense enough not to pry when she hadn't volunteered her reason for making all those trips to California. He'd ventured a guess about the screenplays and known from her tone of voice that he'd hit a dead end.

So he could wait a little longer to find out the rest. She'd given him a huge gift by telling him about her parents. But my God, *Owen Drake.* Big stars competed for the right to be in an Owen Drake movie because it was a good bet to sweep the Oscars. And he didn't want to tell Molly, but he had his own personal copy of *The Haunted Lagoon.* Molly had definitely inherited Cybil O'Connor's red hair and fabulous body.

"So you never wanted to act?" he asked, deciding he could ask questions within the boundaries of what she'd already told him.

"No, never. Mom and Dad tried their best to make me into a star, and as a kid I wanted to please them, so I tried. And failed. I'm way too introverted. I'd throw up before every screen test."

He rubbed his thumb over the back of her hand.

"You seemed like you were having fun when we made that video."

"I did have fun," she said softly. "Because it was for the two of us. I'm not so bad at one-on-one."

Alec chuckled. "You're outstanding at one-on-one. I've never met anybody better."

"But I want you to know, I'm not...like that normally. With a guy, I mean. After hearing what my agent had to say, I made a conscious decision to be more... adventurous."

Desire washed over Alec in warm waves. He forced himself to keep his attention on the two-lane road that curved through the Connecticut countryside, passing wooded areas, quaint villages and white clapboard homes. He'd decided to take the scenic route to Mystic instead of the turnpike, but all he cared to see was the woman sitting next to him. "Are you telling me that I've been treated to a side of Molly Drake never before revealed?"

"Pretty much."

"That makes me feel very special." *And very aroused.* He'd never been excited about the Mystic shopping trip, but right now he was totally without enthusiasm. He would follow Molly anywhere, but if he had a choice, he'd rather follow her to the bedroom then down the aisles of a curio shop.

"You are special. That's why I knew you were the one to take on this adventure with me. I...uh...sort of used you as a model for my hero."

"You *did?*" He found himself flushing with pleasure and feeling very unsophisticated for doing it. "Since when?"

"Um...since soon after you started driving for me."

"Get outta here! You've been using me as the model for your hero for *months?*"

"I hope you're not angry, Alec." She spoke quickly, nervously turning her straw hat around in her lap. "Nobody will ever know except you, but if the idea that I've written those sex scenes and basically used you as my prototype embarrasses you, then—"

"Are you joking? I'm not embarrassed, I'm enormously flattered! I even read some of your book, but I had no idea that you were putting me in that role." He paused, thinking back over what she'd written. "I'm not that good-looking, for one thing."

She smiled at him. "Yes, you are. But it's very cute that you don't think so. And I love the way you're blushing. It makes you even cuter."

"Now you *are* embarrassing me." But in a good way, he thought. Having a beautiful woman pay him compliments was something he could get used to. "Are you supposed to be the heroine in the book?" The entire subject fascinated him.

"Well...not really. I mean, she's prettier, and gutsier, and—'

"No on both counts. She just has different-colored hair. You're as gutsy as they come, Molly. And as beautiful, too."

"Alec, you don't have to say that."

He glanced at her, admiring how the sun coming through the window created sparks of light in her red hair and gave a luminous glow to her skin. She was like a fine painting by one of the old masters. With regret he turned his gaze back to the road. "If I said anything different, I'd be lying. You're gorgeous. I can't believe you haven't had a million guys say that."

"If anyone ever did, I couldn't trust he was telling me

the truth. People would say anything to me if they thought it would get them in good with my father."

"Well, I don't give a diddly-damn about getting in good with your father, so you can trust me. You're amazing. When I saw you come out of the cottage today I got dizzy looking at you."

"That's because you were feeling sexually deprived," she said, laughing.

"Maybe I was, but that's—"

"I would have looked good to you, no matter what."

"Is that why I looked good to you? Because you were sexually deprived?"

"No, that's not why." She grinned at him. "I was sexually deprived, too, but I can be objective. You're a hunk."

"Maybe not." He smiled back at her. "Maybe once you've become thoroughly satisfied by numerous sessions in bed, you'll wake up and discover I'm uglier than Quasimodo."

"I don't think so. I—oh, there's a used bookstore! Could we stop?"

"Sure." He'd been wanting to stop for miles. A secluded country lane would have served him better, but if she wanted to go into a used bookstore, he could deal. Maybe she'd find a couple of rare first editions for her parents and they could bag the Mystic trip and go back to her cottage, back to her bed, back to playing Adam and Eve minus the fig leaves.

The Book Nook was a low, rambling building with enough character to be interesting and enough peeling paint to make Alec think that business was slow. No other cars were parked outside, but the sign in the window next to the door was turned to Open. A tabby cat slept beside the sign. At first Alec thought it might not be real, but then he saw a whisker twitch.

After spending most of Thursday and all his spare time Friday in the law library, he wasn't particularly interested in browsing through some old books, but he could understand why a writer would want to. At this point, whatever Molly wanted, Molly would get. He hoped before too long it would be him, naked.

She left her hat on the seat of the Blazer but brought her purse after announcing that she'd never left a used bookstore without buying at least something. "I can't resist places like this," she said as they approached the front door, which was slightly ajar.

And I can't resist you. Alec put a hand on the small of her back, guiding her through the door even though she was perfectly capable of going inside on her own. "Because of the bargains?"

"Because of the hidden treasures," she said over her shoulder as the bells hanging from the back of the door jingled. "And the smell of books." Inside she took a deep breath. "Ahhh. Now that's heaven."

The place smelled musty to him, but if she liked musty, maybe he'd take down a few books from the shelf and rub them behind his ears.

An older man wearing thick glasses, a striped shirt and pants held up by red suspenders came through the doorway to the left of a battered sales counter. "Well, well. I was thinking I might have to close up early if nobody arrived, but here you are."

"Here we are," Molly said in a voice filled with good cheer.

The man adjusted his glasses. "I'm going to guess you're not from this area."

"I live here now," Molly said, "but I was born in California."

"From the way you talk, I was going to say someplace on the coast," the man said, nodding.

"Maybe eventually I'll sound like a Yankee." She gestured to Alec. "He does."

"I do?" Alec had never given much thought to how he sounded.

"Definitely. Your vowels are more clipped than mine. Don't you think I sound different from you?"

He thought she sounded wonderful, especially when she was whispering in his ear while they were writhing on the bed together. "Well, of course you do. Your voice is softer, nicer."

The old guy laughed. "I have a couple of lovebirds, I see. Spring is in the air."

Alec glanced at Molly to see how she was taking that comment. *Lovebirds* sounded like more than a temporary arrangement. He discovered her looking right back at him, as if that label didn't bother her a bit. His heart beat faster.

"I'll leave you two alone to browse," the man said. "My name's George, so if you need anything, just call out. I'll be in the back room watching *Matlock*."

Molly blinked in surprise. "But you have all these..." Then she paused, as if maybe she shouldn't be commenting on his choice of leisure activities.

"Books?" he finished with a chuckle. "Oh, I read those in the evenings, after I close. I can't read while the store's open because I get so involved in the story, I wouldn't hear the customers come in."

"Oh." Molly nodded in understanding. "That makes perfect sense."

The whole conversation left Alec in the dust. He'd

never been that caught up in a book, but then he'd never had time to read for pleasure, either. He wondered if maybe he'd been missing something.

George started to leave, but then he turned back. "By the way, with you being from California, you might be a Dana Kyle fan. I just got two copies of her latest. They're on the far wall, in the display rack. If you haven't read it, I'd recommend you pick it up. She gets better and better."

"Uh, thanks. I have read it."

Alec was surprised at the change in Molly. It was subtle, and anyone who wasn't as tuned in as he was might have missed it. But she was no longer relaxed.

"Don't you think it was her best one so far?"

"Maybe. Maybe so." Her jaw tensed slightly.

The old guy smiled. "You don't sound like a rabid fan. I'm a rabid fan. I buy her new in hardback, and believe me, I don't do that often. Anyway, I've talked enough. Go prowl around and see what you can find that you can't live without."

"Thanks," Molly said.

Then, to Alec's astonishment, she wandered over to the display rack on the far wall and picked up the Dana Kyle book she'd already read. Alec walked over to stand beside her. There had to be a personal connection to make Molly act this way. He figured she must have history with Dana Kyle, who was, after all, from the world of Hollywood.

"I take it you don't like her?" he asked.

"No, I do, actually. She's a good person."

"Then you must not like her books."

Molly glanced up at him, the book open in her hand. "Why would you think that?"

"No enthusiasm. When you like something, you show it. I should know."

She gazed at him, her green eyes holding back secrets. "I like her books. I just wouldn't say I loved them."

"I wouldn't say so, either. In fact, I can't imagine why you would read them, considering how lukewarm you seem to be."

"Let's just say I have a certain obligation."

"So she *is* a personal friend." He felt the distance between them looming larger. First he'd discovered that she was the daughter of a world-famous director, and now he was learning that she was close friends with a well-known actress who was also a bestselling author.

"Yes, she is."

"Then couldn't she help you break into publishing?" The minute he said it, he could tell from her expression that he'd stepped over the line. "Sorry. That is none of my business. I have no idea what goes on in Hollywood, and you know very well how everything works. I shouldn't—"

"Alec." She put her hand on his arm and spoke gently, almost pleadingly. "It was a logical question to ask. I just can't answer it, okay?"

He looked into her eyes and thought what a fool he'd been to think they would ever be more to each other than bed partners. Even that would run its course soon, and then they'd never see each other again. She might have told him a few things about her life, but she wasn't about to let him in on everything. He'd only be allowed so close and no closer.

She put the book back and took him by the hand. "Don't let this come between us," she said, tugging him between the shelves, away from the sounds of George's television. "Don't let this spoil our time together."

He didn't want that, either. He wanted to be the kind of guy who lived for the moment and let tomorrow take care of itself. That was how they'd begun this caper, and that's how they should continue it.

Unfortunately, he was falling in love with her, which naturally led to thoughts of tomorrow, and of...well... forever. He wasn't sure if he could block out those thoughts and concentrate on the excellent sex they could enjoy right now. But he would try.

He smiled at her and let her lead him around the corner until they were surrounded by rows of old books. "Now, that would be dumb of me, wouldn't it? To pass up a great day of fun and games because I had to know everything about you first?"

She looked uncertain. "I wish I could tell you more, but—"

"Forget about it." He changed the dynamic, tugging her toward him instead of allowing himself to be pulled along. They were far enough into the bowels of this store that George wouldn't be able to see or hear them. "Kiss me, Molly."

Immediately she looked less worried and more devilish. "You want to make out in the bookstore?"

He drew her closer and locked his hands behind her back. "I want to make out anywhere I can get away with it. And you said you loved the way these old books smelled. I thought maybe it got you hot, being back here, surrounded by them."

"You get me hot." She wiggled against him, nudging his erection. Then she wrapped her arms around his neck and stood on tiptoe. "Come here, you."

Being an obliging guy, he leaned down and let her

mouth connect with his. Mmm. Much more of this and he might get hooked on the scent of old books, himself.

He'd been without the taste of Molly for too many hours, and he couldn't seem to get enough of kissing her. God, how he ached. Breathing hard, he cupped her bottom and brought her in as close as he could, considering they were both wearing way too many clothes.

As he began to think they'd better vacate the premises and look for a lonely country road, she slipped her hand between them and neatly pulled down his zipper.

Omigod. Reaction sizzled through him as he lifted his mouth from hers. "Molly?"

"I'm going to turn you into a book lover," she murmured, working his penis free of his briefs.

He gasped. "Listen, old George could—"

Her breath was warm, her breathing as ragged as his. "I checked my watch when he went back there," she said as she continued to fondle him. "The show's on for another fifteen minutes." She slid slowly to her knees. "And this won't take that long."

He should stop her. He really should stop her. But he wasn't going to. Instead, he was going to stand there shaking, threading his fingers through her silky hair and inhaling the scent of old books while she...oh, damn, she had that tongue thing down perfectly, and the suction was...*good*. Unbelievably, wildly...good.

Then he was gone, lost in space as he clenched his teeth and fought to keep from yelling. Oh, geez...incredible, beyond incredible. He felt wobbly as a three-legged table by the time she tucked his still-quivering penis inside his briefs and zipped his fly.

Sliding back up his body, she cupped his head in both hands and gave him a long, erotically flavored kiss. He held on to her for dear life, afraid if he didn't, he might crumple to the floor.

Her deep kiss turned into playful nibbles. "Like that?"

A weak chuckle was all he could manage. No woman had ever tried anything remotely like this, and now he wondered how he could live without the woman who was ready and willing to play such exciting games.

"Want to buy a few books?" she whispered.

"I want...to buy the whole...damn store."

"I don't think George would sell." She trailed kisses over his chin and down his throat. "He loves it here."

"Me, too."

Laughing softly, she stood on tiptoe again and kissed him on the nose. "Now we really do have to buy some books. Will you be okay if I let go of you?"

He opened his eyes and took a deep breath. "I think so. I have to say, this place smells terrific."

"Told you." She gave him a final kiss on the mouth and stepped away from him. "Start shopping."

"Right." He turned toward the nearest shelf and began pulling down dusty books.

She glanced over at him, a book in her hand, and smiled. "You might want to pick things you'll actually read. Unless you have a fondness for that particular part of *Britannica*."

I have a particular fondness for you. He glanced down at the books he held, and sure enough he'd pulled out the middle three volumes from a complete set of encyclopedias. He put them back.

"So what have you got?" he asked, walking over to her on legs still rubbery from the orgasm she'd given him.

"An old copy of *The Joy of Sex*."

Vicki Lewis Thompson   169

"Well, don't get that!"

She grinned at him. "Why not? It has great pictures. See?"

"I see, all right, and if you go up to the counter with that book, George will know something's up."

"Something was." Her green eyes sparkled.

"And if we don't get the hell out of here, it will be again. Let's just grab some books and go."

"Okay, here." She thrust *The Joy of Sex* into his hands. "You buy that, and I'll take these." She took down three more books from the same shelf.

Alec finally noticed the label above the shelf: Human Sexuality. Sure enough, Molly had more books along the same lines as the one she'd shoved off on him. "Molly, I can't go up there and—"

"Why not? I dare you. Tell me, is there a single thing wrong with good sex?"

"No."

"Then why be afraid to let somebody know you like it? Besides, George took these books into his store and created a shelf for them. Do you suppose he would have done that if he never expected anyone to buy them?"

She had a point. He thumbed through the book. It did have some excellent pictures. Now, that pose, right there—

She closed the book before he could read the description. "We can look at them later. Let's go home."

That got his attention. "Home? What about Mystic?"

"I've lost the urge to shop."

"Thank God." Taking her elbow, he propelled her to the front of the store so fast she had to skip to keep up with him. "George?" he called out. "We're ready to pay up and leave."

George ambled out from his hideaway. "Find everything you needed?"

Alec wondered how much George knew about what had just gone on in the back of his bookstore. "Sure did." He placed his book squarely on the scarred counter. "I'll take this one."

"Now, there's a classic," George said, scooting the book over near the cash register so he could flip open the cover and read the price written inside. "No couple should be without this book. Good choice." He rang up the sale on his antique cash register and glanced over at Molly as if wondering if hers would be on the same tab.

Alec decided they would be. They were used books, for Pete's sake, not Waterford crystal. He took Molly's books from her before she realized what he was about to do. "And these, too."

"But—" Molly stepped forward.

"My gift to you." Alec smiled at her.

She looked flustered, but she didn't try to talk him out of it.

"More good choices," George said. He rang up Molly's three books and gave Alec the total.

As Alec was paying for the books, he felt great on several counts. Obviously the sexual episode in the back of the store had put him in a good mood, but having the guts to buy these books made him feel kind of triumphant, too. Last of all, being the one who paid gave him a big boost. Shallow though it might be, he needed that for his masculine pride.

"Here you go, honey." He'd added the endearment on a whim and found he liked the way it sounded. As he handed Molly the stack of books, he wished she'd picked out a few more. They weren't expensive, so it seemed as if he'd given her a lot of stuff.

"Thank you, Alec." Her smile trembled a little at the corners, as if his gesture had touched her.

Well, good. And now it was time to get back to the cottage and touch her in a few other ways. He put his arm around her waist. "Now, let's go home."

13

ON THE WAY BACK to Old Saybrook, Molly admitted to herself that she was in really deep this time. In front of the bookstore owner Alec had treated her like his girl, and that's what she wanted to be. She wanted to share everything with him, including her secret life as Dana Kyle's ghostwriter.

But she couldn't tell him about that, not without getting Dana's okay. Maybe it was a good thing that she was scheduled to see Dana next week. She'd talk to Dana about Alec and ask for permission to tell him about the ghostwriting. She and Alec couldn't have a real relationship until he knew about it.

In the meantime, he needed what she was providing today—lots of fun and sex. He worked very hard, and she didn't think that was good for him, either, especially since he didn't particularly seem to enjoy school. Next Tuesday she'd be leaving for several days, so he could catch up on his work then.

She kept looking for the right moment to mention that, but instinctively she knew it could cause a problem. He would want to know why she was going, especially now, when they'd become so involved with each other. So she was putting off that moment. Knowing she had to tell him about Tuesday's trip was another reason to keep things light between them and not get into any more discussions about her parents and life in Hollywood.

Fortunately her creative behavior in the back of the store seemed to have taken his mind off that subject for the time being. She shouldn't have picked up the latest Dana Kyle in the first place, but she'd been curious to see what George was charging for it. More than he was asking for *The Joy of Sex,* as it turned out. That gave her some satisfaction.

Whenever someone praised the Dana Kyle books in Molly's hearing, she wondered if she should just keep on writing them and forget about her own career. She might never reach that level of readership and fame on her own. But then she'd look around at all the well-stocked shelves in a store like George's and know that she wouldn't rest until at least some book, somewhere, had her name on the spine.

"So are we going to have Saturday night at the movies?" Alec asked as they drew closer to the turnoff for Old Saybrook.

Molly thought of all the things they'd done in front of the camera, and heat rose to her cheeks. She wasn't sure she could sit through the videos with Alec without being mortally embarrassed.

He glanced at her and his eyebrows lifted. "What's this? Hesitation from a woman who performed oral sex in the back of a bookstore, a woman who challenged me to buy sex books in public without flinching?"

"What if we look ridiculous on the tape?" *Or you look terrific and I look like a creature from outer space?*

"What if we look hot? What if it inspires us to do more of the same?"

Molly laughed. "I don't think we need much inspiration. Plus, we have these books."

"C'mon, Molly. Don't wimp out on me, now. I've been dying to see what that video looks like. Let's order a pizza, pick it up on the way home and eat dinner in front of your TV while we watch the tape."

"If we look really stupid, can we shut the whole thing off?"

Alec grinned. "I figure we'll watch maybe three minutes before we start ignoring what's prerecorded and go live. So I wouldn't worry about it."

"Oh." Molly had been trying to control her urges all day, and an image of them having sex on the floor while their filmed selves went at it on-screen was enough to bring her needs bubbling to the surface. "You could be right about that."

"I'm right." He took his cell phone out of the holder on the dash of the Blazer. "What's the number of your favorite pizza place?"

She gave it to him and he punched in the numbers with his thumb.

"What do you want on it?"

"The works."

"See, I knew we were meant for each other."

Molly wished he wouldn't say things like that, comments that a boyfriend would make. While he ordered, she mulled over that phrase. Maybe they were meant for each other, if they'd been lucky enough to meet when they actually had time to find out. Catching moments here and there, how would they ever know?

"Forget I said that." Alec disconnected the phone and put it back in its holder.

She pretended not to understand. "Said what?"

"That we were meant for each other. I was kidding around. I know this is a temporary, for-the-hell-of-it kind of relationship."

If only she could contradict him. "We're not ready for more right now."

"You're right. I could hardly expect you to put up with a couple of hours here, a couple of hours there, not to mention my ever-shrinking budget."

That hit her wrong. "Alec, money isn't an issue. Time, yes, but not money."

"That's because you have plenty."

Here it came, the rich girl–poor boy deal she'd struggled with all her life. Except now she was on her own, not living off her parents' wealth. "I wouldn't say I have plenty."

"Well, you're ahead of me. You own a house—"

"Inherited from my grandmother." But she had to admit not many people her age were handed an entire house, mortgage-free.

"And somehow you manage to buy food and pay for a car service without having a job."

"I—" She stopped herself before saying that she didn't pay for the car service but that she certainly had a job.

"It's okay. I don't blame you for taking money from your folks so you can work on your novel. I'd do the same thing in your shoes. And if somebody gave me a cute little house like that, I'd definitely live in it. I'm just saying that you're way ahead of me on the wealth curve."

She couldn't deny any of that without revealing things she wasn't free to expose. But he was right that she had more money than he had. "And that bothers you."

"Not for the short run," he said quietly. "For the long haul it might."

"But it shouldn't!"

He glanced at her. "Molly, I was raised blue collar, and some of the values stick to me like burrs. I'm giving it to you straight. I don't know if I could date a wealthy woman unless I was knocking down a big salary, myself."

"You have the potential to do that eventually."

"Yeah, but I'm not doing it yet." He pulled up in front of the pizza parlor. "And that said, the pizza's on me." He turned off the engine and hopped out. "Be right back."

She knew better than to try to change his mind, about the pizza or about his old-fashioned ideas concerning money. Ironically, his fierce independence was something she cherished about him. Too many guys had seen her as a contact who would help make them rich.

But she hadn't thought their financial differences would become a solid barrier between them. Maybe she could get him to see that his contribution to her writing career was worth more than a fat bank account. If she hit it big and he was part of the reason, why shouldn't he share in the rewards? Unfortunately, she wasn't sure that argument would fly with someone like Alec.

Even discounting the sale of her own books, she was doing well because of the ghostwriting. He wouldn't be able to match her income for several years, and he'd just said he didn't want anything permanent with a woman who was worth more than he was. By the time they were economic equals, assuming that happened someday, they could be miles apart, both geographically and mentally.

Maybe she never should have started this. But then she would have missed out on some of the most amazing loving she'd ever had. *Loving.* The word described what had happened between them far better than *sex*, yet it was the first time she'd allowed herself to use it.

She watched Alec come out of the pizza parlor carrying a flat cardboard box, and her heart squeezed at how gorgeous he was. Oh, damn, she wanted this connection, no matter what label it should have, to go on forever. And now she was afraid that it might not happen.

When he opened the door and handed her the warm pizza box, the air became saturated with the scent of onions, tomato sauce and melted cheese. A hunky guy and fresh pizza. Throw in a lifetime together, and voila. She had all she needed. But she had to be careful about setting her heart on it.

"I'm starving!" she said. "I didn't realize I was so hungry!"

"Didn't you eat lunch?" He buckled his seat belt and started the engine. "I should have asked you that, but I thought for sure you would have."

"Did I eat lunch?" She had to think about it. "I guess not. I was so excited about you coming over that I forgot all about it, apparently."

"Now, that kind of talk could turn a guy's head." Alec pulled back into light traffic and headed for Molly's cottage.

"Then I'm glad I confessed. You don't give yourself enough credit."

He glanced over at her, his smile warm. "Neither do you, Miss Molly. I didn't bother with lunch, either."

"Because you washed and waxed the truck instead," she guessed.

He shrugged. "It needed to be done."

"You could have picked me up in a dirty old rattle-trap, you know."

"No, I couldn't. That would make it seem as if I didn't give a damn, and that wouldn't—" He stopped speaking abruptly. "Well, I just couldn't."

Her heart beat faster. In other words, he did give a damn. In other words, he was getting as hung up on her as she was on him. In that case, she would start her campaign to help him see that he'd made a major contribution to her writing career.

She cleared her throat. "Before you leave tomorrow, I hope you'll have time to read my revised love scenes. I think they're a lot better. I'll bet Benjamin will think so, too. And I have you to thank for that."

"I'll make the time," he said. "You're going to be a big success, Molly. Bigger than your friend Dana Kyle."

"I'd be satisfied to be half as successful as that." So he'd brought up Dana again. He was probably using their former tense conversation about Dana to remind her that there were secrets between them. He had to be frustrated with her silence, but no matter how much she wanted to tell all, she couldn't. Not until she'd made that trip to California and cleared it with Dana.

BY THE TIME they'd settled on the floor with the pizza box on the coffee table and the TV ready to roll the tape, Alec thought he had his head on straight regarding Molly. His function in her life was similar to a sparring partner for a boxing champion. She'd probably always be grateful to him, but they would never be equals. And love couldn't exist without equality. He knew that.

His heart, however, wasn't listening. His heart wanted to carry Molly off the way Tarzan had carried Jane, and keep her with him in some tree house where they'd make love, have children and grow old together. His heart didn't care that she belonged to another world and was destined for fame and even more fortune than she already had.

As he bit into a fragrant slice of pizza and waited for the snow to clear from the screen, he told his heart to shut up. In a few minutes he'd have the opportunity for some outstanding sex. He'd been so sure of that, he'd laid out a couple of condoms next to the pizza box, which had made Molly laugh.

He'd told her they'd need them, guaranteed. Considering they were about to watch themselves having sex, he was convinced they'd be engaging in more of it in short order. No sense in having mushy thoughts about love and forever mess up what was a very good thing.

"Okay," Molly said as the first image popped onto the screen. "This is me, just lying there, waiting for you to come through the bedroom door." She pulled a slice of pizza from the box and dragged it free of a few cheese strands.

"You look like every man's wet dream." Alec forgot to chew as he stared at Molly lying on the bed. Sure enough, his penis started to get happy.

"I shouldn't have crossed my legs. I look nervous." She took another bite of her pizza.

"Were you?"

"Oh, yeah. My heart was beating like crazy. Can't you hear the squeak in my voice when I called out to you?"

"I can't pay attention to your breasts and your voice at the same time, and I'm more interested in your breasts. Your breasts are very photogenic."

"Gee, thanks. Whoops, here comes the man of the hour. Now we have dialogue."

"What dialogue? I'm just staring at you like one of

those cartoon guys with springs on his eyeballs. I look like I have the IQ of a dust bunny."

That made her laugh, which he was glad for. She seemed way too tense, when he was hoping this viewing would loosen her up. He really did look like a doofus, though, standing there ogling while he took off his clothes. "Geez, did I actually start interviewing you about your video experience? What a nerd."

She laughed harder. "You did. You sounded like a regular Tom Brokaw. *Were you a film student in L.A.? A starlet?* Meanwhile you were getting out of your clothes like they were on fire. So there I am, trying to slow you down."

"And there I am, giving you a little of my life story. I'm about to have my first taped sex ever, and I have to pause to explain that I chop wood for the landlady for a break on the rent. This video needed a scriptwriter, bad."

"I'm liking it so far." Molly giggled and finished off her first piece of pizza.

Alec groaned as he watched himself fumbling with his belt. "Get the prong out of the hole, dummy. You do it every day of your miserable life, but when you're on camera, you suddenly can't remember how it goes."

"I thought it was cute that you were so excited."

"Cute, my ass. Too bad you decided to share the set with a long lost cousin of the Three Stooges. I—" He stopped, the slice of pizza halfway to his mouth. She'd started fooling around with his belt. He stared at the screen as his groin began to throb. Slowly he laid the pizza slice back in the box without taking his attention from what Molly was doing with his belt.

"I can't believe I really did that," she murmured.

"Mmmph." It was the best he could manage as he

concentrated on the screen version of Molly using that belt in a way he'd never imagined a belt being used. He'd never told her, but that belt was rolled up and enshrined in the back of his sock drawer, never to be worn again. He thought of it with more reverence than his Mike Piazza autographed baseball.

Back and forth the belt slid, and Molly moaned softly. He moaned, too, both on-screen and off. Then she made herself come. Oh...my...God.

"Alec..." Molly laid a hand on his thigh.

That was all it took. He shoved the coffee table aside, urged her down to the braided rug and started wrenching away clothes, both his and hers. Wild cries on the video spurred him on. He had to have her now, this minute, or he would start babbling like a madman.

"Quick!" She was gasping, obviously as hot as he was.

"I'm trying!" He ripped her panties in the process of getting them off. He didn't care. Then he somehow got his fly open and the condom in place, while his screen self and the screen Molly continued to groan and thrash about. As if that weren't enough to send him over the edge, the real Molly began pleading with him in the most explicit language he'd ever heard from her, which inflamed him even more.

By the time he rose over her and plunged deep, he felt like a sex maniac. "Is this what you want?" he cried, stroking her hard.

"Yes! Like that! Oh, Alec, I'm coming! I'm *coming.*"

So was he, in a rush that made his ears buzz. This was living.

MOLLY FELT AS IF they were hosting an orgy. The tape continued to run while they recovered from their first frantic session. They took a long hot shower together, deliberately not making love because they both knew there was more video in store. By the time they were ready to start watching again, Molly in her satin bathrobe and Alec with a towel knotted around his waist, their on-screen counterparts were once again writhing on the bed.

Before long, Molly and Alec were making love on the sofa, accompanied by parallel groans and moans coming from the television set. "Stereo sex," Alec murmured in her ear as he stroked slowly in and out.

"Are you watching?"

"No." He lifted his head and gazed into her eyes. "I'd rather watch the real thing. But listening is kinda fun."

She felt her orgasm hover nearer with each thrust. "So you don't think...we should shut it...off?"

"Are you crazy?" He shifted his angle and found her G-spot. "Tell me you're not turned on by hearing us at the same time we're doing it."

"I am." She clutched his hips and lifted to give him deeper access. "I don't know what kind of woman that makes me, but I am."

"That makes you my kind of woman." He looked into her eyes as he pumped faster. "I should take that back." He gasped. "But I won't."

She had to give as good as she got. It was only fair. They couldn't tell each other the truth, but they could edge close to it. "Then...let me say you're my...kind of man." Breathing hard, she kept her gaze locked with his.

His focus sharpened. "Molly, I—"

"Don't say anything you can't take back." She stopped him before he could confess too much. It was still too soon for declarations of love.

Longing flashed in his eyes, then was gone. Pressing his lips together, he increased his speed. She closed her eyes and abandoned herself to pure sensation as he took them both over the edge and their cries of release blended with the ones recorded on the tape.

Holding him close, Molly trembled in the aftermath of her climax...and battled regret.

ALEC TRIED NOT TO LOVE sleeping next to Molly through the night. He tried to squelch the rush of joy he felt waking up in her bed and the contentment that poured over him as they shared bagels and coffee and the Sunday paper. She showed him her staged ending to the video, an ending they'd been too involved to see the night before. They replayed it about ten times, laughing like fools.

The clock marched on, but he did his best to ignore it. Time was his enemy today. After all, a guy couldn't be blamed for wanting to linger in paradise.

He read her revised love scenes, which caused them to act out another one. Once again he had to swallow the words that came so naturally while he was deep inside her. Her revised scenes were damn good, and as he thought of that, he realized that he'd done his job. Theoretically, after today she might not need him anymore.

But he refused to believe she'd drop him that quickly. Maybe they were both skating on thin ice, trying to enjoy what they had without letting it become more, but he had to believe she wanted to continue as much as he did. She wasn't faking happiness. After all these hours with her, he'd know.

Still, he stayed as long as he dared, afraid to break their magic connection again. Finally he had no choice but to put on his clothes in preparation for heading out the door.

"I have classes all day tomorrow," he said. "I wish I could cut a few, but I'd better not."

"I wouldn't want you to." She'd pulled on a T-shirt and a pair of short denim coveralls that transformed her into a sexy country bumpkin.

She looked so adorable that Alec had a tough time imagining he wouldn't see her the next day. "Unfortunately I also have a driving assignment tomorrow night. I could come by afterward, though, because I'm free on Tuesday. Maybe we could have a picnic down on the beach. Maybe—"

"Alec, there's something I need to tell you about Tuesday. I've put it off because...because I don't like it any better than you will."

His stomach twisted. Whatever was coming, he wasn't going to be happy about it. "What's that?"

"I have to go to L.A."

The twisting in his stomach grew worse. "I didn't see it on the Red Carpet schedule." He had the irrational thought that if he hadn't seen it there, it couldn't be true.

"I know." She rushed through the rest. "I forgot to call, which was stupid of me because by waiting until the last minute like this, I was taking a chance that you wouldn't be available, and I don't want anybody but you taking me to the airport."

"I'll take you to the airport." He felt as if he'd eaten a serving of steel filings for breakfast, and he couldn't seem to move, either, as if he'd become magnetized to the spot by all that metal. "How long will you be gone?"

"I..." She clenched her hands together in front of her

and her eyes were filled with anxiety. "I don't know. I'll have to call for...for a pickup, but I'll make sure it's on a day you don't have class."

Her distress finally broke the spell her words had cast over him, and he moved forward to pull her into his arms. "Molly, tell me why you're going to L.A." He cradled her head against his chest and stroked her silky hair. "I can see you don't want to. Maybe there's something I can do about it."

She hugged him fiercely and kept her face buried against his shirt. "There's nothing you can do. And I can't tell you why I'm going. I wish I could, but I can't."

"I hate this."

"I know. Me, too."

"Okay." With a sigh he forced himself to let her go. "I can still come by on Monday night and then go back for the limo early Tuesday."

She shook her head, her gaze sad. "I have things to do, Alec. I'll need the time between now and then to get everything done."

This just wasn't getting any better, no matter how he tried. "Then I'll see you Tuesday. What time?"

"Eight."

He nodded. "You'd probably better call in, so Edgars doesn't get suspicious. I probably shouldn't tell him you made the reservation through me."

"I'll call right after you leave."

He cupped her face in both hands and gave her a long, searching kiss. All he learned from it was that she wanted him as much as he wanted her. For whatever good that did. And then, finally, he had to go.

"See you Tuesday," she called after him.

"Right." He walked out the door. How quickly paradise could become hell.

14

MOLLY STOOD hugging herself, a lump in her throat and an ache in her heart as she listened to Alec drive away. Putting off telling Alec about the ghostwriting didn't feel right. He thought she was deliberately shutting him out of a part of her life, and that had to feel really horrible to him. But she could see no other way to handle this. She couldn't say anything until she'd talked with Dana in person. Considering that she'd never asked to reveal the secret to someone, a phone call wasn't enough.

In the meantime, she had plenty of writing to do if she expected to show Dana several chapters of the new mystery, a mystery in which the supposedly kindly old gardener was really the killer. And she had to pack, and call her parents, and generally get back to being Molly Drake, daughter of Owen and Cybil, ghostwriter for Dana Kyle. For a few sweet days she'd been someone else—Molly Drake, budding novelist and sexual adventurer—but her other life demanded her attention now.

First on the agenda was calling in her request for a chauffeur from Red Carpet Limousine. Hard to believe the last time she'd asked for Alec, he'd been scheduled to take her to the train station so that she could keep her appointment with Benjamin. It seemed weeks ago instead of days. Now everything had changed.

She was seriously considering a relationship with

Alec. Maybe if she stayed in California until his finals were over, they could spend the summer together before he had to immerse himself in school again. Sure, he'd still be taking a chance dating her while he was working for Red Carpet, but she could solve that by buying a car and learning to drive. Alec would probably say she didn't need to, but unless he would accept gas money, she wasn't about to let him take her everywhere in his Blazer.

The prospect of a summer devoted to writing and Alec made her much more cheerful as she crossed to the telephone table, picked up the receiver and dialed the number she knew by heart. She'd never called Red Carpet on a Sunday before, and she wondered if they'd have the phones switched to voice mail. To her surprise a man answered, and a second later she realized why he sounded familiar.

"Josh?" she said. "This is Molly. I didn't expect you to be answering the Red Carpet phone."

"Something went haywire with our voice mail, so we're rotating the phone detail. What can I do for you?"

Because Josh knew about her and Alec and probably didn't approve, Molly stumbled with her request. "I would like—ah—I need a ride to JFK on Tuesday. Um, Tuesday morning at eight. Please."

"Sure thing," Josh said smoothly. "I guess you're requesting Alec, as usual." Keys clicked in the background as Josh accessed her file on the computer.

"Yes."

"Does he already know about this?"

Molly hesitated, not sure what to say.

"It's okay, Molly." Josh sounded much kinder than he had the last time he'd talked to her. "I'm not going to turn in one of my best friends. And when I couldn't get him all day yesterday or last night, I thought he was probably with you."

Guilt washed over her. "Was it urgent? Because you could have called here, Josh. I wouldn't have minded that."

"Not earthshaking. I had a date Friday night with a girl from one of his classes and I wanted to check with him on a couple of things."

"He worked really hard Thursday and Friday so he could take a little time off." Molly heard the defensive tone in her voice and took a deep breath. Josh wasn't Alec's keeper, and she didn't have to justify anything to him.

"I'm sure he did. And you probably think I should butt out of his business."

"I don't know if you should or not," she said honestly, less confident than she'd like to be. "He tells me he has everything under control."

"Let's hope he does. Megan didn't seem to think so. She said he was on thin ice to begin with because of all the hours he works. She said I should tell him to get his butt in gear because next week is critical. A paper's due, plus they'll be reviewing for the final. Now, we're only talking about one class, here, but it's an important class, one he needs to graduate."

"I won't be a distraction next week because I'll be in California." Molly decided to trust Josh. Alec obviously did. "In fact, I was thinking I might stay there until the end of the semester."

There was a brief pause. "That would be a good idea, Molly."

Josh sounded so parental that she felt compelled to defend Alec. "On the other hand, I'm sure he has the discipline to complete his class work, even if I'm here."

There was an even longer silence this time. "You've known him six months, but I've known him eighteen years. Don't get me wrong, I love the guy. But if he doesn't figure out what to do with his life pretty soon...well, I hate to see someone with all that potential bouncing around the way he has. And I'm just a friend. His folks are ready to tear their hair out."

Molly felt sick to her stomach. Everyone was worried about Alec's future, and here she came, creating a distraction he obviously didn't need right now. "Well, hasn't he finally settled on being a lawyer?"

"That's what he says, but I've seen this pattern before. He gets to a point when it looks as if he really might grab hold and make a career of something, and then he finds some reason not to give it his full attention. Usually it's because he's helping someone else."

Like her, with her book. She closed her eyes in dismay.

"When he was in architecture," Josh continued, "he got involved in helping a buddy build a cabin up in Maine. During the premed phase he was on some orientation tour at the hospital and met an old lady with terminal cancer and no relatives nearby. He took her on as a project, and let his studies slide."

"I can picture him doing that." Molly's throat felt tight at the thought of Alec's soft heart and innate goodness. But she wasn't a dying old woman, and she couldn't have him sacrificing that way for her.

"I'm not saying that wasn't wonderful, what he did for that lady, but it's almost as if he looks for these distractions. I thought he'd made it over the hump and was really focused on getting his law degree, but..."

"Now he's helping me with my book."

"Exactly. I understand there's more to your relationship than that, but his behavior the past few days has been classic, and I hate to stand by and watch him throw another promising career down the drain."

She fought against the inevitable conclusion. "He hasn't done that yet. You might be worrying prematurely."

"I might, but in the past, once he loses his enthusiasm, he never goes back to the original program. He shuts that door and looks around for another option."

Well, there it was. She didn't have much choice now. Bracing herself for what was to come, she took another deep breath. "I can promise you one thing, Josh. If he closes the door on his law career, it will have nothing to do with me."

"I'm glad to hear that. Listen, the other line's ringing, so I'd better answer it. Nice talking to you."

"Same here," she lied, and disconnected the phone. Nothing about the conversation had been nice. Josh had informed her that she was poison to Alec's future, and from all the evidence, she was.

She'd foolishly imagined they could enjoy the summer together, but she'd been sadly mistaken. If Alec spent a summer critiquing her sex scenes and encouraging her writing, not to mention all the lovemaking they'd enjoy in between, what were the chances he'd want to dive back into his law studies?

Molly knew the answer to that question. In order to become a lawyer, Alec would have to force his way through some hard and maybe even boring months of school. She didn't know if he'd do that or not, but she would keep her promise to Josh. If Alec dropped out of law school, it wouldn't be her fault. She wouldn't do that to the man she loved.

ALEC DIDN'T LIKE the idea of Molly going to L.A. Actually, he hated it. He'd always hated it, he realized, even before they'd become lovers, but now the separation would be almost impossible to bear.

But he would bear it, and he'd work like a demon in his classes while she was gone so they could have even more time together once she came back. He wished she'd set a time when she'd be home. Okay, maybe she considered L.A. home because her folks lived there, but he thought she belonged in Connecticut. With him.

This summer they'd work out all the kinks in their relationship. After all, they'd only been dating for a few days. He couldn't expect her to tell him everything she'd been keeping quiet about after only a few days. Over the summer she'd let him into her private world. He was sure of it.

So although he didn't look forward to having her gone and didn't want to drive her to JFK this morning, he'd look on it as a necessary step, a way to mark off some days before their long and very hot summer arrived. As he parked the Town Car in front of her cottage, even though the sky was overcast and rain threatened, he was almost cheerful.

Molly didn't run out to meet him this time, but that was okay. She might still be packing. And he was determined not to ask her anything about the reason for this trip, either. No sense in pushing now when they'd have all summer together.

As he stepped up on the porch, she opened the door, and he caught his breath, stunned as always by how beautiful she was. She'd dressed for comfort in low-slung black slacks and a cropped black knit shirt that showed off her tiny waist and flat stomach. He envied every single person at JFK who would be treated to the sight of Molly Drake this morning.

"Come on in for a minute." She stepped back from the door.

He laughed, more than happy to oblige. "Is that a good idea? You might miss your plane."

She didn't smile back. Instead, she wrapped her arms around him and gave him a long, soul-shattering kiss.

He moaned and pulled her closer, forgetting everything but the need to hold her, kiss her, make love to her, no matter what the consequences might be.

Apparently she wasn't as swept away, though, because she wiggled out of his arms and backed away. "We...we have to go."

He couldn't help wishing that maybe she'd change her mind. Maybe she'd say to hell with the trip and spend the day here with him. "Are you sure? That kiss felt more like hello than goodbye."

"I'm sorry."

He took a closer look and realized her eyes glistened. She was close to tears. His heart constricted. She was leaving, honoring whatever obligation she had back in L.A., but she didn't want to go.

He decided to make it easier on her. "Hey, don't worry about me. I'll be hitting the books while you're gone. Your timing is good, as a matter of fact. I found out yesterday that I need to put my nose to the grindstone this week."

She swallowed. "I'll bet you do."

"Hey, by the time you get back I'll have everything squared away." He couldn't stand looking into those sad eyes another second, so he glanced around and located her suitcase sitting by the front door. "Let's get moving, Miss Molly." He grabbed the designer luggage by the handle and carried it out the door, the way he had countless times before in the past six months.

Except this time everything was different. This trip he'd chauffeur a woman he'd made love to for hours, a woman who could change the color of his world with her smile.

She wasn't giving him any of those smiles today, though. She continued to blink away tears as he helped her into the car and stowed the suitcase in the trunk. He climbed into the car and looked over at her. She had her hands clenched in her lap and her jaw was tight. She looked as if she'd like to roll into a ball and shut out the world.

"It'll be okay, Molly." He rubbed his hand over her knee. "It's only for a little while."

She nodded, not speaking and not looking at him.

With a final squeeze, he turned to the business of driving her to the airport. "Music?" he asked as they pulled away from her cottage.

"No, thanks." Her voice was thick with unshed tears.

"You keep this up, I'm liable to start bawling, too, and then where will we be?"

"I'm...I'm sorry." She sniffed. "Go ahead and turn on the CD player if you want."

"That's okay." He focused on the road ahead. "We can just drive."

And drive they did, without a word being exchanged. Alec was enormously flattered that she was this upset about leaving him. Maybe all his wild daydreams about building a life with her weren't so out of the ballpark, after all.

Finally, as they neared the airport, he decided to test the waters. "You know, I won't be in class this summer."

No response.

"I have to work for Red Carpet and make money, of

course, but that won't take all my time. We could have
a great summer, Molly. I'm thinking of simple things,
like roasting marshmallows on the beach, taking a ferry
ride, or just lying in the sand counting the stars. Doesn't
that sound good?"

She made a funny little noise in her throat, as if she
might be choking back a sob. He hadn't meant to make
her feel worse, so he gave up on that tactic. She must *really* be upset.

He had another horrible thought. "Molly, are your
folks doing all right? Nobody's real sick, are they?"

She shook her head.

"That's good. I was worried that you might have gotten some bad news recently." Strange. If nobody was
dead or dying, she was reacting to this trip with more
emotion than he would have expected.

"Tell you what," he said as they approached the terminal. "Do you still have my card with the cell number
on it?"

She gave no indication she'd even heard him, although she must have.

"Anyway, here's another one." He pulled it out of the
clip on his visor and handed it to her. "Call me anytime
while you're out there. And I mean anytime. I wouldn't
even care if you woke me up. I'll probably be dreaming
about you, anyway." He swung the Town Car neatly
into a spot by the curb and unfastened his seat belt so he
could get out.

"Alec, wait."

For one wild moment he thought she might ask him
to keep driving and take her back to the cottage. But after a quick look at her tear-streaked face, he knew that
wasn't happening. "Molly, honey, what is it?" He
started to cup her face in his hands, but she drew back.

He stared at her, unable to believe that she'd pulled away from him.

"It's over." She drew a ragged breath. "It's over between us, Alec."

He sat there stunned, waiting for the pain to hit him. Instead, he felt numb, incapable of moving or speaking.

"This is goodbye."

He saw her lips move, even interpreted what she'd said, but he couldn't hear her over the roaring in his ears.

She snapped open her seat belt and reached for the door. "If you'll pop the trunk latch, I'll get my suitcase. You can stay here."

The sound of her door opening penetrated the static in his head, and he grabbed her arm before she could leave. "You can't be serious." His voice came out in a croak, as if he'd been sick for a week.

She gazed at him, tears dribbling out of her eyes. "I'm serious. When I get back, whenever that is, I'll find a new car service. I'm sorry, Alec, but that's the way it has to be."

"Bullshit!" He gripped her arm tighter. "You feel something for me! Look at me and tell me I mean nothing to you!"

"You mean a great deal to me."

"Then for God's sake, why?"

"Because it's best. Please, Alec, let me go."

"Best for who?" In his agony, he dredged up the only reason that made sense. "Is there someone in L.A.? Someone who has a hold on you?" *Or someone you need more than me?*

"No."

"Then, damn it, why can't we pick up where we left off when you get back? I can't believe you're dropping me because you've figured out how to write your sex scenes so now I'm dispensable. You're not that kind of woman."

She swallowed. "Thank you for that." Then she looked down at his fingers wrapped securely around her arm, and back into his eyes. "You need to let me go, Alec. I'll miss my plane."

His throat felt raw. "Isn't there anything I can say, anything I can do, that will change your mind about this?"

She shook her head.

"Maybe you'll decide differently once you get to California. Keep my card. Call me. We'll talk about this." He sounded frantic, but he couldn't worry about his pride right now.

"I won't change my mind. Don't hold out any hope that I will. That will only make things more difficult."

"They couldn't be more difficult."

"Alec..." Her glance was pleading as she glanced again at the arm he continued to clutch desperately.

He let her go. Obviously nothing would make a difference now, but he refused to believe this was the end. No matter how many times he'd told himself they'd part ways eventually, he hadn't really faced the possibility. And after Saturday and Sunday, when they'd been so happy, so good together, he'd pushed it completely from his mind.

Operating on autopilot, he unlatched the trunk and made it around to the back before she did. He'd be damned if he'd let her wrangle her own suitcase. He lifted it out, set it on its wheels and snapped the raised handle into place. Only then did he turn it over to her.

"Goodbye, Alec," she said.

He'd started to feel reckless by then. "Where's the kiss to go along with the kiss-off?"

"That was...back at the cottage."

"Yeah, but I didn't know that then." Stepping quickly around the suitcase, he caught her chin in his hand and gave her a fierce kiss, thrusting his tongue deep, claiming that right whether she wanted him to or not. Then he looked into her eyes. "This is not the end," he murmured. Turning away, he walked back to the driver's side of the limo, got in and closed the door.

The pain hit him then, and it was far worse than he'd expected. For a few seconds he was afraid he might embarrass himself and throw up. Somehow he maneuvered the big car out into the thick traffic of the passenger drop-off area without hitting anybody. He wasn't fit to drive, but he had no choice. He headed away from the terminal, using every ounce of discipline he had to keep from wrecking the car, even though right now he didn't care about the car or himself.

But eventually the pain would ease enough for him to be able to think. He had to believe that or go crazy. Then again, maybe he was crazy already, because despite all the reasons why he wasn't fit to wipe Molly's shoes, he was determined to see her again. No matter what she'd said, they were a long way from being over.

15

ONCE BACK in her parents' Beverly Hills mansion, Molly decided she was a better actress than she'd thought. She'd convinced both her mom and dad that although she might seem depressed, she was merely exhausted from a heavy writing schedule.

After a rare family dinner that made her feel unusually nostalgic, she excused herself and escaped to her old room before she spilled her guts. She knew her parents, and they would beg her to move home again. She didn't feel strong enough to fight that battle.

Once upon a time her bedroom had felt like a prison. A pricey prison, for sure, with its huge canopied bed, adjacent marble bath and a balcony that looked out on an Olympic-size pool, but a prison nevertheless. Decorated in artfully faded denim and a sunflower print, the California-chic designed room was an expression of what her parents had wanted for her more than her own vision. She'd always preferred Grandma Nell's cozy antiques and ruffles.

But for now, she was glad to be in this room instead of at the cottage. Eventually she'd go back. She wasn't about to give up her beloved cottage because of painful memories. She'd learned to accept that Grandma Nell wasn't there anymore, so she'd learn to accept that Alec wouldn't be there anymore, either.

Flopping down on the king-size mattress, she turned

over and stared up at the giant sunflowers splashed on the canopy. Well, she'd done the noble thing where Alec was concerned. She hadn't attempted that many noble deeds in her life, and she was disappointed that this one left her feeling so crappy. She should feel uplifted by the knowledge that Alec could now realize his full potential, thanks to her stepping aside.

Instead, she kept picturing his face when she'd delivered the blow. She'd made him suffer, and even though it was supposed to be for his own good, she hated thinking of how he would continue to suffer, at least for a while. He didn't deserve that.

She'd considered delaying the bad news until she flew back to Connecticut, but she was afraid the longer she waited, the less courage she'd have to actually do it. After being away from him for a week or two, she would have been so glad to see him that she wouldn't have been able to say those necessary words. She might never have said them.

And he would have given up his plan of being a lawyer. She truly believed Josh was right about that. Once she'd taken off her rose-colored glasses, she'd seen all the signs that he was headed in that direction. Feeling horrible now was better than finding out later that she'd unintentionally sabotaged Alec's dream.

She sure hoped Josh would be able to talk some sense into Alec and make him see that breaking up with her was in his best interests. Thinking of Josh sharing a beer with Alec and comforting him made her feel a little bit better. Yes, Josh would take care of Alec.

As for her, she needed to make her mind a blank so that she could get some sleep. At the moment that seemed like an unreachable goal, but she'd count as many sheep—or sunflowers—as it took. Tomorrow included her lunch with Dana, and for that she had to be sharp if she expected to convince Dana that the gardener did it.

ALEC HAD THE DAY FREE. He spent it in the law library, but his books lay unopened in front of him. Once again, he was at a crossroads in his life, and this time he was going to make the right choice, the choice he should have made a long time ago. Finally, when he had the plan that made sense to him, he gathered up his books and went back to his apartment.

He was on the Internet when his doorbell buzzed later that night. His ancient computer was so damn slow that he could easily answer the door while he waited for the site to come up.

Josh stood on the other side of the door, a six-pack in one hand. "I came as soon as I could." He walked in and headed for the kitchenette. "Let's pop the top on a couple of these and you can tell me all about it. Or we can watch the ball game on TV and not talk about it. Whatever you want."

"I'll be with you in a minute. Let me take care of something on the computer first."

Josh's eyebrows rose. "You're working on that paper already? You da man!"

"Uh, no. Something else. Open a beer for me, would you?" He wanted Josh to have a brew in his hand before hearing the news.

"Sure. I thought I'd open several for you before the night's over. I'm glad to see you at the computer, though. That's an excellent sign."

Alec went back to his small computer desk and started making choices on the screen. At one point he reached in his back pocket, took his credit card out of his wallet and punched in those numbers. There. Done. His printer started whooshing and groaning as it coughed up a receipt. Alec closed the window of the travel site before Josh came over, a beer in each hand.

He glanced at the credit card lying beside the computer. "You buying something?"

"Yeah." Alec took the beer Josh handed him and stood. "Thanks."

Josh clicked his can against Alec's. "To the future."

"I'll drink to that." Alec took a hefty swallow, and some of the butterflies in his stomach mellowed out. "Have a seat." He gestured toward the tweed sofa. "Oh, and I hate to back out on taking that Saturday gig for you, but I don't think I can do it."

"Hey, not a problem." Josh settled onto the sofa. "You have a tough schedule coming up. I probably shouldn't let Pris think I'm a coward, anyway. Besides, there will be bridesmaids, right? I could end up with a couple of phone numbers out of the deal."

"There's a thought." Alec knew how committed he was to Molly when the idea of collecting phone numbers left him totally cold.

"Listen, do you want something to eat?" Josh asked. "I didn't think about it until I was pulling into the parking lot, but maybe I should have stopped for a pizza. Knowing you, you haven't had anything to eat all day. We could still call in an order."

The thought of pizza got those butterflies flapping their wings again. He couldn't think of pizza without remembering the one he'd shared with Molly Saturday night. "That's okay. I'm not hungry."

"We can always decide later." Josh glanced at his watch. "We've got an hour before they close."

Alec forced himself to sit in the armchair across from

Josh, although he would rather walk around while he talked. Adrenaline pumped through him.

"This is for the best, man," Josh said. "I know you don't think so now, but it is."

Alec gazed at his friend. He suspected that Josh had talked to Molly and influenced her decision, but he didn't plan to ask. No doubt Josh thought he was justified. Alec wasn't about to create more tension by confronting him.

Josh shifted his weight on the cushions. "The main thing is to get back on track, here. Don't let this throw you. The semester is almost over."

For me, it's completely over. But he had something to discuss with Josh before saying that. "I want to talk about your limo business."

"You mean the one where you'll do pro bono legal work for me?" Josh grinned.

Alec leaned forward. "I'd rather help you run it, Josh."

"Run it? You won't have time for that. The legal advice is one thing, but you wouldn't be able to—"

"I want to be partners with you. That is, if you'll have me. I'm a little cash-poor right now, but I'll do my best to catch up before the day comes when you're ready to sign on the dotted line. If I'm not quite ready, I'll float a loan."

"I don't get it." Josh frowned. "I know there's a bowling alley lawyer on TV, but I can't picture you running a law practice out of a limo, man."

"I don't want to be a lawyer. I want to run a car service, just like you."

Josh groaned and flopped back on the sofa, almost spilling his beer. "Jesus, Joseph and Mary. I give up. You know, I really give up."

"Listen to me, Josh. All these years of school, I've—"

"No, I don't give up, damn it!" Josh jerked forward again, and this time he did slosh beer out of his can and onto the sofa. He didn't seem to notice as he pointed a finger at Alec. "You are the smartest guy I know! And your folks are so proud of you! I thought your mom was going to needlepoint and frame your S.A.T. scores. And your dad, boy does he want to see you make good. That man—"

"Exactly. I have been in school, trying to find a profession that would make *my dad* happy. I never stopped to think what would make *me* happy. And you know what I love?"

Josh rolled his eyes. "You have no idea what you love. You're so tied up with this woman you can't think straight."

"That's not true, Josh. I'm thinking straight for the first time in my life. I've seen how much Molly loves her writing. I met this guy who runs a bookstore, and he might be poor, but God, he's happy."

"Poor but happy. Now, there's a goal."

"Maybe it is! I love driving. I love meeting new people, people celebrating happy events. How many happy people does a lawyer see in a day?"

Josh blew out a breath. "You're in it for the bucks, not the yucks."

"Then that's the wrong damn reason. I want to be partners with you and own a fleet of limos. We could have a blast."

Josh sat there slowly shaking his head. "I've watched you go from this to that to the other thing for years now, but this is the dumbest idea I've ever heard come out of your mouth."

"Does that mean you wouldn't want me as a partner?" Alec's shoulders sagged. He could create his own business, of course, but being partners with Josh would be more fun, and then they wouldn't be in competition with each other.

Josh ran a hand over his face. "No, that's not what it means. If you were some average-IQ Joe, with all your other endearing traits, I'd be honored to be your partner. But you were meant for greater things."

"I can't think of anything greater than doing a job I love and being business partners with a good friend."

"That's so sweet. And so dumb. Listen, you—"

"No, you listen." Alec took a deep breath. "I've hated school all these years. I hate school as much as you do, but I've stayed with it because I thought I had to, to please my dad. As you might have noticed, I couldn't force myself to actually finish any of those degrees."

"I noticed."

"See, Molly's folks wanted her to be a movie star, but she stuck to her guns and became a writer, instead. I needed to hear that kind of story, I guess, to give me the courage to go for what I really want."

Josh looked down at his beer can, turning it around and around in his hands. Finally he glanced up again. "At least finish out the semester. Then you can think about this over the summer. This is too big a decision to make it so fast."

"It's too big a decision to put off another second. I can't finish out the semester, Josh. I'm leaving tomorrow morning for California."

Josh gaped at him. "You're not."

"Yes, I am. I'm going after Molly."

THE NEXT DAY AT NOON, a maid ushered Molly out to the deck of Dana's Malibu home. Beyond the deck's redwood railing, the Pacific Ocean glittered under a warm sun. Next to the railing, a wrought-iron table shaded by a large umbrella was set for lunch. A vase of roses sat on the table, and the scent taunted Molly with the memory of Alec, bringing her a single red rose....

"Molly, sweetheart!"

Molly turned, dredged up a smile and walked into Dana's arms for a hug. In between visits she always forgot how small Dana was and how fragile she felt through the multicolored layers of chiffon she loved wearing at home. On the silver screen Dana was a commanding presence, but in person she looked as if a strong wind would blow her off the deck.

Dana took both Molly's hands and stood back to gaze at her. "You're looking beautiful, as always. Very smart in your halter top and hipster jeans. Oh, for the days when I could wear that kind of outfit."

Molly laughed as she looked at Dana's unlined face and cap of dark curls. "Come on, Dana. You could wear this outfit and get wolf whistles."

"Sure, down at the rest home! Now, let's eat. I'm famished." She led Molly to the table as if she were five years old. "Irma, bring the food and the martini pitcher!"

Five was how old Molly had been the first time she'd stood on this deck. In the middle of a cocktail party, Dana had brought out a pack of cards and played Go Fish with her youngest guest. Molly had been Dana's slave ever since.

"So, how are things in Connecticut?" Dana asked as the maid served crab salad and sliced melon.

Molly sipped her martini. Dana's house was the only place where she drank them. Maybe it was the martini. Maybe the scent of roses got past her defenses. In any case, the words came out before she could stop them. "I met someone."

"You *did?*" Dana's famous blue eyes gleamed with interest. "Is he wonderful? Well, of course he's wonderful, or you wouldn't have given him the time of day. When do I get to meet him?"

Before Molly could stop herself, she was blubbering into her crab salad and confessing the whole miserable story. Dana made sympathetic little noises and rubbed her back until Molly finally sputtered to a stop and wiped her eyes on her linen napkin.

"I didn't meant to blurt all that out," she said, sniffing and looking at Dana through watery eyes.

"Of course you did." Dana gave her a squeeze. "I've had more than my share of experience in this area, sweetheart, so I totally understand heartbreak. Are you absolutely positive that this young man—Alec, is it?"

Molly nodded.

"Are you quite sure that Alec couldn't become a lawyer *and* be involved with you?"

"It looks that way. He has a history of giving up on his studies when something more interesting comes along."

Dana smiled. "I'm sure you're more interesting than any old textbook, but darling, in my experience, which is considerable, if a man wants to become a doctor, or a lawyer, or, heaven help us, an actor, nothing will stop him, not even a beautiful woman. Woman are more easily distracted by love than men. Trust me on this."

"Lust," Molly said.

"Pardon?"

"He was distracted by lust. I don't know that love factored into it."

"Ah. But it did with you, didn't it, sweetheart?"

Molly nodded again.

"So you made the ultimate sacrifice. I wonder if he'll let you do that."

"He might. For one thing, I'm afraid he thinks I have a boyfriend here in California."

"Why on earth would he think that?"

Molly took a long, shaky breath. "Because I never told him why I come out here so often. So, naturally he could assume—"

"Well, you need to tell him why."

Molly blinked. "Just like that? You don't even know him. We've kept this secret so well because nobody knows except you, me, my folks and Benjamin. I think it's risky to add another person to that list."

Dana sighed and settled back in her chair. "I think it's risky to keep secrets from those we love. I've been wondering if I need to tell Jim." Her cheeks turned pink. "We might start living together, and I couldn't very well keep up the charade, but I'm wondering what he'll say."

Molly reached over and squeezed her hand. "Tell him the truth. Tell him we work together on the books."

Dana gazed at her. "No, we don't, and you know it. I've only pretended that. You write them, Molly. I only kibitz."

Something in Dana's expression made Molly bold. "Dana, what would you think if…if we made this the last book we did?"

Relief flooded her features. Then she quickly concealed it. "I couldn't do that to you. You have a career going."

"I want to write under my own name. I think I can do it. No, I know I can."

Dana's eyes widened. "Oh, thank *God.* I've been

wanting to wrap this up, especially with Jim on the scene, but it's been so good for you, and I didn't want to take away your chance to write for a living." She picked up her martini glass. "Here's to the retirement of Dana Kyle, bestselling author, and the rise of Molly Drake, a new publishing star on the horizon."

"I can't believe this. Are you sure you want to end Dana Kyle's career as a writer?"

"Yes. And look, darling, *something* has to work out for you. If it can't be love, then maybe it can be your career. Now, toast with me. To your success."

"All right." Smiling, Molly clicked the rim of her glass against Dana's. "To success." As she drank, she thought about Dana. She had a career most women would envy, but she'd lost her true love and had spent years searching for the right man to share her life. Molly hoped she wasn't doomed to repeat that pattern.

THE HOME OF OWEN DRAKE and Cybil O'Connor wasn't listed on the tourist map labeled Homes of the Stars, and Alec knew better than to try the phone book. Finally he figured out the answer. In a Tom Hanks kind of move, he walked into a florist shop in Beverly Hills and paid an obscene amount of money to send flowers to Molly Drake, daughter of Owen Drake.

He admitted to the counter clerk that he didn't know where the Drakes lived, but he added a large tip with the understanding that the florist would know. The clerk promised that the flowers would be delivered. Alec included a note telling Molly that he'd be in the cocktail lounge of the Beverly Wilshire Hotel at six that night, if she was willing to see him.

The hotel was an instinctive choice—it was where they'd filmed *Pretty Woman.* He was looking for all the good karma he could find, and if the place had worked for Julia Roberts and Richard Gere, it might work for Molly Drake and Alec Masterson. It was the best he could do.

For the rest of the afternoon he walked along Rodeo Drive carrying his small gym bag and wondering if he might run into Molly coming out of one of the shops. He didn't see Molly, but he was positive Jennifer Aniston walked past, and he could swear the guy getting into the Jag parked at the curb up ahead of him was Hugh Jackman.

No doubt about it, Molly lived in a completely different world here in California. But she'd given up this life for her grandmother's cottage in Old Saybrook. He kept reminding himself of that to shore up his courage.

At five-thirty he went into the hotel lounge and ordered himself an imported beer. He didn't feel right sitting at one of the raised tables with a domestic brand in front of him. Money was flowing out of his pockets in a steady stream, what with the last-minute plane ticket, the cab ride from LAX and the flowers. Fortunately Josh had agreed to let him buy into the business with sweat equity when the time came.

As he sat nursing his beer, he thought about what he had to offer Molly. Not much. Looking at his financial picture nearly made him pay for the beer and leave. But he couldn't do that. He was through giving up on things. Now that he'd decided what he needed in his life—Molly and a business partnership with Josh—he was going after them, no matter how scared he was.

At ten minutes to six, Molly arrived, her face pink with fury. The rest of her looked wonderful, though, with her cute little halter top and low-slung jeans. She slammed her purse down on the table and climbed onto a stool across from him.

He loved her so much, he couldn't manage to say a single word.

She could, though. "Exactly *what* do you think you're doing here? What about your exam? What about your paper? What about—"

"Us?"

"You're doing it, aren't you?" She was quivering with anger. "You're giving up being a lawyer because of me. So help me, Alec, I—"

"No, not because of you."

Her jaw dropped and she seemed to momentarily stall out.

"Molly, I love you, but that's not why I'm giving up on becoming a lawyer."

"It is so! You're using me as..." Her eyes widened and she gulped. "Wait a minute. What...what did you say, again?"

"I love you, but that's not why I'm—"

Tears filled her eyes. "You love me?"

"With all my heart. And you love me."

Tears streamed down her cheeks. "No, I don't. Not if it's going to mess up your life."

Finally he gave in to the need to touch her. He reached over and took her hand in both of his. This was how they'd begun, holding hands across a table, deciding to spend the afternoon in a hotel room together. Or maybe they'd begun the first time he'd laid eyes on Molly Drake.

She used her free hand to swipe at her eyes. "Alec, go back to Connecticut. You're so smart, you can still save your semester if you take the next flight and get right to work."

He smiled and squeezed her hand. "You're making my point for me. Only a woman who really loves a man would give him up, even though she wants him so much it makes her cry."

"I'm no good for you!" She grabbed the napkin from his side of the table and wiped her nose. "Don't you see that?"

"I see that you're perfect for me. I only hope that after I tell you what I've decided to do with my life, you'll decide I'm perfect for you."

She wiped her nose again and sniffed. "You'd make such a good lawyer. And you've already studied so hard to get to where you are. I can't stand the idea of you quitting now."

"Maybe you will after you hear what I have to say." Speaking carefully, he explained everything, beginning with his parents' hopes for him from the time he was in grade school to his bungled attempts to fulfill those hopes. He'd always thought he was persuasive, which was the reason he'd decided to give law a try. He hoped to hell that he could be persuasive now.

At last he'd laid his case in front of her. He'd even mentioned George, the happy bookstore owner. He paused, his pulse racing, and waited for her reaction.

"What does Josh think?"

"That I'm an idiot. But I'm counting on you to understand. Your folks wanted something different for you, too."

Her fingers tightened in his. "Alec, on that subject, there's something I want to tell you about why I've been coming to California so much. I—"

"It doesn't matter. If it's a boyfriend, then you'll just have to get rid of him. Because you're going to marry me. I'm the right guy for you, as long as you don't mind being married to somebody who chauffeurs people around for—"

She launched herself in his direction, nearly toppling the table and his beer as she came off her stool and pulled him off of his. "I love you!" She grabbed him and kissed him with such enthusiasm that he grew dizzy and had to hold on to her really tight. At last she paused to take in some air.

"Wow. I guess you do love me." Alec wasn't about to let go of her, but he wondered what the patrons of the bar were thinking of this display. Well, they were in Hollywood, so maybe it wasn't all that unusual.

Then again, maybe they were attracting some unwanted attention. From the corner of his eye, Alec saw a twenty-something kid sidling up to them.

"Excuse me." The kid addressed Molly. "But aren't you Owen Drake's daughter? I forget your name, but I remember the red hair."

Molly turned and gazed at the guy for a long moment. "No. I'm not."

"Are you positive? You look exactly like her."

Alec's arms tightened possessively. "Actually, she's Molly Masterson, the writer."

Smiling, Molly glanced quickly into Alec's eyes. "I hadn't thought of that."

"Personally, I like the sound of it."

Joy danced in her green eyes. "Me, too."

"Hey, I've never heard of a writer named Molly Masterson," the kid said.

"You will." Alec glared at him. "Now, scram." He thought he sounded like Robert De Niro, the way he said that. Hollywood was getting to be a fun place.

With a shrug, the kid left.

Molly continued to gaze up at him adoringly. "So

you really don't want to hear why I've been making all these trips to L.A.?"

He did, but she seemed to like knowing that he'd take her, secret and all. "Someday. When you're ready to tell me."

She looked so happy, she glowed. "That's how I know you love me. You'll take me, anyway."

"I'll take you any way I can get you." He leaned down and kissed her again, just to make sure this was all real. Then he gazed into her eyes. "And you're sure it's okay that all I want to do is be partners with Josh in the limo business?"

"More than okay." She cupped his face in both hands. "And you can drive Molly Masterson, the writer, anywhere, anytime."

He held her close and pictured all the years of loving this amazing woman. The moment needed a good, movie-style line to make it complete, and he had just the one. "I think—" he paused and leaned down to feather her mouth with his "—that I'll just drive you wild."

___EPILOGUE___

A year later

FOR A WOMAN who was exhausted, sweaty and unbelievably sore, Molly felt damn good. Alec stood by her hospital bed holding a swaddled Cybil Denise, named after her two grandmothers. Denise, the new grandma, was going crazy with the camera, while Alec's father, Jerry, couldn't stop grinning, and his sister, Lauren, kept begging to hold the baby.

Alec didn't look as if he'd hand her over anytime soon. He stared at his daughter with such adoration that Molly decided she'd have to be the disciplinarian in the family. Cybil's daddy would give her the moon and a golden box to put it in.

With the way things were going with A Sweet Ride, the new car service he and Josh had launched six months ago, baby Cybil would be showered with presents from her daddy. Neither of the men could have predicted that their old boss would declare bankruptcy, leaving the customer base to flounder. Josh and Alec had moved swiftly to open A Sweet Ride, buying up the limos at auction so the business was ready to roll in under a month.

Molly hadn't seen much of Alec since then. She'd consoled herself with a particularly hot memory. Nine months ago he'd surprised her with an impromptu trip into the city and an amazing night in the same hotel room where they'd first made love. Molly was positive that was when they'd created Cybil Denise.

Alec had promised that once the baby came he'd cut back on his hours. From his awestruck expression as he gazed at his child, he wouldn't have any trouble keeping that promise. Molly looked forward to having Alec around a little more. Other than the carpenters adding a second bedroom onto the cottage, she hadn't had much company recently except for the characters in her new book.

"Come on, Alec," Lauren begged. "Give her to me. You have those father-of-the-kid things to do, like call everybody you know and brag on your ability to reproduce."

"I do wish you'd call my parents," Molly added gently. "And Dana. And Josh. And Benjamin."

"Benjamin?" Alec frowned. "Can't we just send him an announcement?"

"No, we can't." Molly laughed, and discovered that laughing hurt. She didn't care. It was so worth it, to be here watching the man she loved more than life holding their beautiful child. "Benjamin specifically asked to be called. He should still be at the office." Ever since Benjamin had trashed her first book, even though he'd since raved over the rewrites, Alec hadn't been able to warm up to the guy.

Alec sighed. "Okay. After I call your folks and Dana and Josh, I'll call ol' Benny." He reluctantly eased Cybil into Lauren's eager arms. "Be careful. Support her head. Don't let her get in a draft. Make sure you—"

"Oh, good grief, Alec." Lauren adjusted the baby in her arms and peered into her wrinkled little face. "You are in big trouble, C.D. Your daddy isn't going to let you do anything fun, so you'll have to—"

"She is *not* going to be called C.D.," Alec said darkly.

Lauren gave him an impish grin. "We'll see. Now make your calls."

Molly tried to stay awake as Alec called both her parents, Dana and Josh. But she was so very tired. She managed to rouse herself long enough to tell them each that she loved them when Alec held the phone to her ear. Then she closed her eyes again while he dialed Benjamin's number.

After what seemed only a moment later, she felt the soft press of Alec's lips against her forehead. Then came his voice, low but urgent. "Molly, *wake up.*"

She forced her eyes open. "Alec, I really need to—".

"Trust me, you want to hear this." He put the cell phone to her ear. "It's Benjamin."

She licked her dry lips and wondered why she had to personally talk to Benjamin. "Hi, Benjamin."

"Congratulations, Molly!" His voice boomed over the line.

She hadn't expected him to be quite so impressed, but she thought it was nice, anyway. "Thank you, Benjamin. She's a beautiful little girl."

"Congratulations on her, too, of course. But let's face it, you don't sell a book every day, either. I think that's—"

"A book?" She was wide awake. "I sold *Jungle Heat?*"

"Assuming you accept the offer I got today, and I would advise you to do that. It's a fine offer."

Molly glanced up and saw Alec gazing down at her, his eyes glowing with pride. "I sold *Jungle Heat,*" she whispered.

"I know." His voice trembled with excitement.

"I sold my book! Oh, Alec. And it's all because of you." Her throat tightened and tears threatened to fall.

"I didn't do anything."

"Yes, you did. You taught me—" She stopped, suddenly aware of the other people in the room and Benjamin still on the line.

Alec smiled gently and took back the phone. "She'll accept the offer, Benjamin. And thanks. We'll be in touch. 'Bye."

Lauren approached the bed holding Cybil. "I'm giving this sweetie back to you, big brother. Mom and Dad and I agree this is an excellent moment to go in search of coffee so you and your new family can have time alone to celebrate all your good fortune." She gazed down at Molly, her glance tender. "That's wonderful about the book. I know how much you wanted that." Then she squeezed Molly's hand and left.

By then Molly's face was wet with tears. "I have a sister now," she told Alec. "Plus a second mom and dad."

"Yep." His eyes brimmed with emotion.

"And I have a wonderful husband, a gorgeous daughter and a book contract. Is there anything left to want?"

Holding Cybil carefully in his arms, Alec leaned down to kiss Molly on the lips. "Only one thing I can think of."

"What?"

Moving closer, he murmured softly into her ear. "Our own video camera."

* * * * *

Molly and Alec are happily settled, but what about Josh, Alec's partner in the limo business? Sparks fly when Josh is forced to chauffeur his ex-girlfriend, Priscilla Adams, to the church on her wedding day.
Look for

DRIVE ME CRAZY,

Vicki Lewis Thompson's sequel to DRIVE ME WILD, *available in April as an online serial at*
www.eharlequin.com.

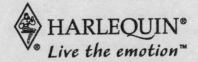

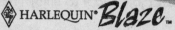

HARLEQUIN® *Blaze*™

GUESS WHO'S STEAMING UP THESE SHEETS...?

It's talented Blaze author Kristin Hardy!

With a hot new miniseries:

Under THE COVERS

Watch for the following titles and keep an eye out for a
special bed that brings a special night to each of these
three incredible couples!

#78 SCORING March 2003

Becka Landon and Mace Duvall know how the *game* is played,
they just can't agree on who seduced whom *first!*

#86 AS BAD AS CAN BE May 2003

Mallory Carson and Shay O'Connor are rivals in the bar business—
but *never* in the bedroom....

#94 SLIPPERY WHEN WET July 2003

Taylor DeWitt and Beckett Stratford *accidentally* find themselves
on the honeymoon of a lifetime!

Don't miss this trilogy of sexy stories...
Available wherever Harlequin books are sold.

HARLEQUIN®
Live the emotion™

Visit us at www.eHarlequin.com   HBBTS

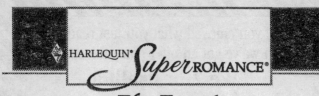

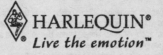

A "Mother of the Year" contest brings
overwhelming response as thousands of women
vie for the luxurious grand prize....

Kate Hoffmann

Jacqueline Diamond

Jill Shalvis

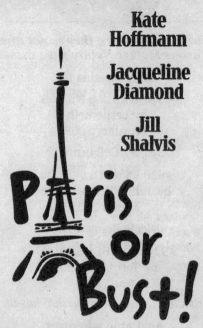

Paris or Bust!

A hilarious and romantic trio of new stories!

With a trip to Paris at stake, these women are
determined to win! But the laughs are many as three of
them discover that being finalists isn't the most
excitement they'll ever have.... Falling in love is!

Available in April 2003.

HARLEQUIN®
Makes any time special ®

Visit us at www.eHarlequin.com   PHPOB

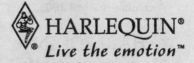